Bikinis
and
Murder

BAREFOOT SLEUTH MYSTERIES

BOOK FOUR

H.Y. HANNA

CONTENTS

CHAPTER ONE

"Are your boobs real?"

Ellie Bishop looked up, startled, then felt a mixture of relief and embarrassment as she realized the question wasn't directed at her. Instead, it was being directed at a girl standing a few feet away, clad in the skimpiest hot-pink bikini that Ellie had ever seen. The few scraps of fabric barely covered the girl's body and only served to accentuate her enormous bust.

Which is probably the point when you're in a bikini contest, Ellie told herself with a smile. As she glanced at the other girl—the one who had asked the question and who also had an improbable hourglass figure— Ellie couldn't help thinking of pots and black kettles...

"Oh yeah, these are a hundred percent natural,"

replied the girl in the hot-pink bikini.

The other girl scowled. "There's no way real breasts look like that," she said.

"And how would *you* know, Amber?" said the girl in the hot-pink bikini, looking pointedly at the other girl's bust.

Amber gasped. "How dare you! You know damn well I've never had plastic surgery. You'd better not be spreading fake rumors about me, Brandi!"

Brandi tossed her head airily. "I can do whatever I like."

"No, you can't! You keep acting like you're so special, like you're better than the rest of us, but you're not!"

"I *know* I'm special," said Brandi, smoothing her hands down her body and emphasizing the curve of her waist and hips. "I'm, like, the only girl here with a thirty-eight-inch bust and that means a lot in a bikini contest." She leaned forward with a smug smile. "It means I'm gonna win."

"We'll see about that!" said Amber, tossing her own hair. She spun around and sashayed away.

Brandi laughed derisively and followed her. Ellie watched them go, both tottering in enormous platform heels, and she sighed wistfully. To her envious eyes, they both had perfect figures: the ideal combination of long, tanned limbs and curves in all the right places. She glanced down at her own body and was pleased to see that in the weeks since she'd arrived in Florida, she was finally beginning to develop a *slight* tan. True, most of her sun exposure seemed to produce freckles rather than that lovely, even, golden glow, but it was still better than the completely pale skin that she had left London with.

Still... Ellie looked up again and took in the group of girls at the front of the catamaran. *Who wouldn't feel a bit insecure when sharing a boat with a group of bikini pageant contestants?* Then she heard a rich, throaty laugh and she looked up at the flybridge to see a spry older woman with curly grey hair sitting and drinking cocktails with a middle-aged man. The woman was eye-catching, not just for her bright eyes and impish smile, but for the fact that she was wearing a lurid red bikini. Ellie smiled to herself. *Aunt Olive, that's who!* she thought.

Trust her aunt to have no issues with confidence despite her age and mature body. Ellie could just hear her mother's shocked gasp in her head and her father's disapproving tones saying: "Wearing a bikini? At sixty-four? Whatever will people think?" But that was exactly the point. Aunt Olive didn't care what anyone thought. She had a complete disregard for conventional expectations and the niceties of society. For years, she had frustrated friends and family as she indulged in a series of romantic flings instead of settling down with a nice, respectable husband to start a family, like all her contemporaries were doing. Then, well into middle-age, she had finally married a wealthy American thirty years her senior who had doted on her and left her a very rich

3

widow when he died several years later.

Not content to rest on her laurels, Aunt Olive had confounded family and friends again when she decided to embark on a new career as a mystery author—and found great success with her books worldwide. In fact, her "celebrity status" had earned spots for both herself and Ellie on the guest list for this boating trip. Don Palmer, owner of Bronzed Babe Sunscreens, which was sponsoring the bikini contest, was a big fan of Aunt Olive's books. When he'd heard that she was staying at the resort where the contest would be held, he had insisted on sending her an invitation—and Aunt Olive had been delighted to accept. Like all writers, she was always up for new experiences which could provide inspiration and research for her stories.

Besides, this was no ordinary boating trip. The bevy of bikini-clad beauties on board were all taking part in the competition to decide this year's "Ultimate Bikini Babe." The winner would receive a lucrative modeling contract as the new face—or rather body— of Don Palmer's company. The girls' excitement was infectious, while their inclination towards high drama was irresistible to someone like Aunt Olive who loved to observe human nature. As for Ellie, she was just delighted by the chance to experience sailing on a luxury catamaran. She had already considered herself the luckiest girl in the world to have her aunt invite her on an all-expenses-paid vacation at a beach resort in Florida, but this was the icing on the cake!

Ellie leaned against the railing now and watched the ocean swells rolling past. The Leopard 58 catamaran cut smoothly through the sparkling waters of the Gulf of Mexico, its gleaming white hull reflecting the mellow light of the late afternoon sun. In the distance, she could see the shore with the beautiful white sand beaches that made this stretch of the Florida coastline so popular. From so far away, the lounge chairs and cabanas that lined the beaches were mere dots, and even the sweeping buildings of the Sunset Palms Beach Resort looked like miniature toy models. Ellie took a deep breath of the fresh, salty air and closed her eyes, savoring the feel of the sea breeze on her face.

"Enjoying the trip, poppet?"

Ellie opened her eyes and turned around to see that Aunt Olive had come down to join her on the aft deck. "Oh, it's fabulous! I've never sailed on a catamaran before—it's much smoother than a yacht, isn't it?"

"Don't let Earl hear you say that," said Aunt Olive with a wink. "He thinks nothing can match his beloved yacht."

"His boat *is* fantastic," said Ellie hastily. "I've had a fantastic time on trips with him—especially that time when I caught my very first fish!" She smiled at the memory. "But this is totally different, isn't it?"

"Well, it's probably even more unusual because of the company we're keeping," said Aunt Olive.

She glanced up at the flybridge where the middle-aged man she had been chatting with was now joined by a couple of girls in skimpy bikinis—more contestants from the pageant, no doubt. The man was smiling complacently and leaning back in the white leather settee to snake his arms around the girls on either side. He had probably been a good-looking man in his youth, but with age, he had developed an enormous beer belly, sagging jowls, and a receding hairline. That wouldn't have been so bad if he hadn't tried to cover up his hair loss with the most ridiculous-looking black toupee. He also had gleaming teeth which had obviously been artificially whitened and looked almost predatory in his fake-tanned-face. The girls beside him seemed oblivious to his appearance, though, as they giggled and flirted with him.

"Amazing what men can get away with when they're rich," commented Aunt Olive, watching the little scene above them.

"Who is he?" asked Ellie.

"That, my dear, is Don Palmer—owner of Bronzed Babe Sunscreens and sponsor of the bikini contest."

"Oh? I didn't realize he was coming on the trip with us."

Aunt Olive snorted. "Do you think he'd miss the opportunity to get up-close and personal with some of the contestants?"

Ellie looked up at the man again. He was turning to one of the girls and brandishing a bottle of sunscreen with the distinctive "Bronzed Babe" label. His voice drifted down from the flybridge:

"...your shoulders are looking mighty red, sweetheart. It's important to keep the sunscreen fresh, you know... here, let me apply some on you..."

"Oh, Mr. Palmer... you're too kind!" the girl simpered.

Ellie watched as the man leaned a bit closer than necessary and smeared sunscreen on her bare shoulder with a lecherous gleam in his eye. The girl didn't flinch, her smile firmly in place as she let Don Palmer touch her, but Ellie couldn't repress a shudder.

"Ugh!" she said under her breath.

"Yes, he's a dreadful, repulsive man," said Aunt Olive.

Ellie gave a shocked laugh. "Aunt Olive! He'll hear you!"

Her aunt gave another snort. "I doubt it. Don Palmer only has ears for one thing and that's his own voice. Trust me, I can tell you from experience."

"You seemed to spend quite a while chatting with him, though," Ellie said.

"Well, I had to, dear. After all, we are his guests and it would have been rude of me to ignore the host. I may be outspoken in private, but I am never bad-mannered in public." Aunt Olive fluffed her grey curls. "In any case, narcissistic egomaniacs can be quite entertaining to listen to, in small doses. And to give Palmer his due, he *is* a self-made man: he started the company with nothing more than a stall at the local market, selling his own formula of sunscreen, and now it's a multi-million-dollar corporation with stores across America. According to the media, that's quite an achievement for a boy from small-town Kentucky."

"And now he's got his own beauty pageant where he has the perfect excuse to ogle and grope pretty young women," said Ellie dryly.

"Yes, although he might not be enjoying that privilege for much longer," said Aunt Olive. "The 'Bronzed Babe Bikini Contest' used to be a big event in the local calendar and was even televised, you know, but ratings have been falling in recent years. Last year, it was dropped from broadcasting altogether, which was a huge blow to Palmer's ego."

"Where did you hear all this?"

"Oh, the resort grapevine…" said Aunt Olive airily.

"Well, I suppose bikini contests aren't very PC nowadays, are they?" asked Ellie, wrinkling her nose. "I wouldn't have thought that any are still being held!"

"Oh, you'd be surprised, poppet," said Aunt Olive. "Bikini contests are still an integral part of Florida's culture and you'll still find dozens of them up and down the state every year."

"Really? I thought they're really controversial."

"Oh, they are. Anything that glorifies an unhealthy obsession with the 'perfect' female body— not to mention all that 'meat-market' ogling—isn't going to be considered kosher in these modern times... but when has that stopped anyone?" asked Aunt Olive with a shrug. She glanced up at the flybridge again. "Palmer told me he's hired a new PR and Events Management agency. That might inject some new life back into the event. Gina Ross is a clever girl and she seems to know what she's doing."

"Mmm," said Ellie in a noncommittal tone. Then, worried that she might have sounded too unenthusiastic she added hastily, "Yes, Gina is fantastic at her job! Just convincing Palmer to hold the contest at one of the top luxury beach resorts in Florida was a brilliant idea. I mean, people always like hearing about aspirational destinations, and having the backdrop of the beautiful resort grounds and the sweeping views of the beach will lift the contest to a totally new level!"

Aunt Olive gave her an amused look. "My goodness, poppet, are you sure you don't want to be working for Gina?"

Ellie flushed. "I'm... I'm just telling the truth. Sunset Palms Beach Resort *is* a gorgeous place and Gina *is* really talented at her job."

Aunt Olive said in a teasing voice: "It's just a shame that she's also your boyfriend's ex!"

"Blake's not my boyfriend," said Ellie quickly.

"Then what is he?"

"He's... We're..." Ellie trailed off, not sure how to describe her budding relationship with Blake Thornton, the handsome resident doctor at the

Sunset Palms Beach Resort.

When she had arrived in Florida a few weeks ago for her extended vacation with her aunt, Ellie had been determined to have fun, enjoy new experiences, and maybe even embark on an adventure or two. But the one thing she'd been determined not to do was fall in love. After all, she had just come out of a disastrous three-year relationship which had ended with her then boyfriend cheating on her. The last thing she needed was to jump straight into another romantic entanglement—especially one that possibly involved a long-distance relationship across the Atlantic!

So Ellie had tried her best to ignore the way her heart jumped every time Blake walked into the room, or the sizzling chemistry she had with the handsome MD. She told herself firmly that it was *just* a vacation fling: nothing more than a bit of fun and diversion until after the new year, when she would bid Blake farewell and head back to "real life" in England.

Besides, things are even more complicated now that Gina is on the scene, she thought darkly.

She had only just gotten over the emotional upheaval she had suffered a week ago when she'd thought Blake was stringing her along while simultaneously seeing another girl behind her back. As it turned out, it had all been a big misunderstanding, but the whole experience had left Ellie even more wary than before. And then Gina had arrived at the resort. At first, Ellie had thought that

Blake's ex had just come for an opportunistic holiday, but it turned out that Gina had also come to check out the location for work purposes. And with her PR and Events Management agency having taken on the job of promoting the Bronzed Babe Bikini Contest, it meant that her visit was going to be a long one...

Ellie shifted uncomfortably. To be honest, she was ashamed of her jealous feelings toward Gina, but she couldn't seem to help herself. Aside from her blonde-haired beauty and perfectly groomed appearance, Gina was also everything that Ellie was not: "grown-up" and sophisticated, talented and capable, the owner of a successful business who knew exactly what she wanted in life and how to go after it... Ellie felt completely inadequate in comparison.

"I didn't realize it was such a complex question, poppet. Shall I come back in an hour?"

Ellie started at the sound of her aunt's teasing voice and looked up guiltily. "Sorry, Aunt Olive!" She sighed. "This is going to sound like a terrible cliché but... it's complicated. Especially now that Gina's here," she added.

Aunt Olive raised her eyebrows. "Blake doesn't seem like he's in a hurry to get back with his ex-girlfriend."

"No, he's not," Ellie admitted. "But Gina's made it clear that rekindling their romance is definitely on her agenda. And she's the kind of girl who will do anything to get what she wants. Anyway, not that it's really any of my business," she added hurriedly. "I mean, it's not like I have any claim on Blake. We've only been out on a couple of dates and we haven't even—" She broke off. She had been about to say "*had a proper kiss*" but that felt somehow too personal a revelation, even to her aunt.

Aunt Olive gave her a shrewd look, but she didn't comment. Instead, she changed the subject, saying: "I'm going over to join the girls and watch the photoshoot. Coming?"

"Yes, all right. But I'm just popping to the loo first," said Ellie, pushing away from the railing.

"You mean the head," said Aunt Olive.

Ellie laughed. "Yes, sorry, the head." She gave a sigh. "I'm never going to get used to all these nautical terms!"

CHAPTER TWO

Ellie went through the large, spacious saloon, with its luxurious interiors and adjoining galley, and down the steps on the starboard side to the companionway below. There was a guest head here, which was shared between the two guest cabins, and she pushed the door eagerly open. But as she was about to step in, she nearly crashed into a girl who was standing at the sink.

"Oh, I beg your pardon!" cried Ellie.

"No, it's my fault—I forgot to lock the door," said the girl, giving Ellie a sheepish smile. "I guess I'm lucky no one came in while I was sitting on the toilet!"

Ellie returned her smile. The girl was extremely pretty, with large, heavily lashed brown eyes that matched her chestnut hair. Like the other contestants, she was dressed in a revealing bikini which showed off an enviable figure. She adjusted her bikini top, glanced in the mirror, then adjusted her top again.

"Do you think I look okay in my bikini?" she asked Ellie anxiously.

"I think you look amazing," said Ellie with genuine admiration.

"Thanks," said the girl with a grateful smile. "I'm Roxy, by the way."

"I'm Ellie."

"Are you with the agency? I didn't see you when Gina was introducing everyone earlier."

"Oh no, I'm just a hanger-on," said Ellie with a chuckle. "My aunt and I are guests of Mr. Palmer, and we're just spectators."

Roxy gave a little sigh and said, "I'm so nervous. It's my first time in a pageant and, well... the other girls all seem so gorgeous and confident! And they're, like, so good with their hair and make-up. I've tried watching YouTube videos and stuff, but I don't know if I'm doing it right." She tilted her face up. "Do you think I look okay?"

"Erm..." Ellie wondered how to answer truthfully without hurting the girl's feelings.

Like a lot of inexperienced young women, Roxy had obviously subscribed to the belief that "more is more." She had been very heavy-handed with the eye-shadow, blush, and foundation, which was caked so thickly on her cheeks that her face almost had a mask-like quality. She had also applied lashings of mascara, so that her eyelashes left sooty smudges against her cheeks with every blink.

"You know, I've heard that the 'natural look' is really 'in' at the moment," said Ellie brightly. "So... uh... maybe it's fine if you don't put on so much make-up. Just let your natural beauty shine through, as they say!"

"Are you English?" asked Roxy.

Ellie laughed. "Yes, is it obvious from my pasty white skin?"

"Oh no, it's your accent," said the girl, smiling shyly. "I love the British accent." She glanced at Ellie's arms, which were covered with a smattering of freckles. "I've got a friend like you. She's also got milky white skin that never tans correctly. But you know what she uses? Fake tan. It looks, like, so realistic you'd never know the difference! Bronzed Babe has a line of fake tans, you know, as well as sunscreen. You should try them out—they smell delicious too." Roxy sighed wistfully. "I'd love to be the model for the line."

"That's the prize if you win the contest, isn't it?" asked Ellie.

Roxy nodded. "Yeah, and prize money, although it's really the contract that all the girls want. It could be the first step to a modeling career! You could end up on posters and billboards across the country, or maybe even, like, in a TV commercial."

"Well, I'm sure you've got as good a chance of winning as anyone else," said Ellie warmly.

A shadow crossed the girl's face. "As long as nothing happens to me," she muttered.

"What d'you mean?" asked Ellie.

The girl looked nervously over Ellie's shoulder, as if to make sure no one else was around, then she lowered her voice and said, "There have been, like, creepy things happening."

"Creepy things?" echoed Ellie, surprised. "What d'you mean, creepy?"

"Well, like... like when Nikki got back to her room last night and found some of her make-up missing, but her roommate swears that she never touched anything. And when we first arrived at the resort, Kimberley found a bunch of flowers addressed to her, which would have been super sweet except they were, like, all dead and dried up, you know? She got all freaked out. I mean, it was like someone had made up a bunch of dead flowers and sent them to her on purpose." Roxy shivered. "And this morning at breakfast, Sharlene said someone had deliberately smeared dog crap on her shoes."

"Did they tell anyone about these incidents?" asked Ellie.

"Yeah, we told Gina, but she just laughed it off and said we were overreacting. She said with the dead flowers thing—someone had probably left the bouquet there too long. And about Sharlene, well, everyone knows she's, like, really clumsy. She's always tripping and falling and stepping on things. Gina said she must have stepped on the dog doo-doo herself and didn't realize." Roxy frowned. "But I don't believe her. I think there's a hex on this bikini contest and I'm scared."

"If you're really worried, why don't you speak to the police?" Ellie suggested.

"No way!" cried Roxy. "They'd probably laugh at me. Besides, I don't wanna be the girl who snitched to the police! That would bring bad PR to the event and Mr. Palmer would hate me! And they say he's real important to the judging of the contest. You know, if he likes you, you get special perks, but if he turns against you, you're out." She straightened her shoulders. "Anyway, maybe Gina's right. Maybe they're just stupid pranks." She took a deep breath and gave Ellie a smile. "I'd better get back out there. I haven't done my photoshoot yet."

"Good luck," said Ellie, adding with a grin: "What's the thing you Americans say? 'Knock 'em dead'?"

Roxy giggled and then, with a grateful look at Ellie, she left and went back topside.

Ellie stepped into the head and shut the door behind her. But as she turned toward the toilet, she made a sound of annoyance. The toilet paper was finished. She looked around the cubicle, opening and shutting cabinets, but could not find any replacements for the bare cardboard roll. Sighing, Ellie stepped back outside and paused in the companionway. She knew that there must be a second head on the other side of the catamaran, although it was probably an en suite linked to the master stateroom for Don Palmer's private use.

But surely it would be OK for me to nip over to use it really quickly? thought Ellie. *After all, Aunt Olive and I are official guests on the boat.*

She made her way across to the port side of the catamaran and was pleased to discover that the en suite head was fully supplied with toilet paper. She had just finished and was washing her hands, when she heard voices in the stateroom outside. They sounded like a man and a woman.

Oh no, not again, groaned Ellie silently. The last time she'd been in an en suite head on a boat, she'd ended up in a humiliating situation, listening to awful cringeworthy endearments from a lovemaking couple outside. The last thing she wanted to do was repeat that experience. Hastily, Ellie dried her hands and prepared to step out and reveal herself before things got too embarrassing. Then she paused as she realized that the man and woman's voices didn't sound affectionate or flirtatious—in fact, they sounded like they were arguing.

It's Don Palmer, Ellie thought suddenly, recognizing the man's belligerent tone. And the female voice belonged to Gina Ross. Don Palmer's angry voice rose and carried clearly to Ellie in the en suite head:

"...you promised when I hired you that you'd turn things around! I can't have another year of poor ratings—the contest could end up canceled altogether. I need more publicity, more buzz about the event," growled Don Palmer.

"Don't worry, Mr. Palmer," said Gina, her voice smooth. "I've got it all covered. This is going to be the most talked-about bikini contest in Florida for a long time to come."

"Oh yeah? I don't see much happening so far," grumbled Palmer. "I mean, what about the media? Why aren't we in all the big papers? What about TV coverage?"

"To get famous nowadays, it's not good enough to be in the traditional media," said Gina. "You have to go viral; you have to dominate social media. No one cares what's in newspapers anymore—people care about the stuff in their Twitter feed or what their friends are sharing on Facebook. You've got to own a hashtag; you've got to start a meme."

"Eh?" Palmer sounded thoroughly confused.

"Trust me," said Gina confidently. "I've got stuff in motion that's going to generate publicity like you've never seen before."

"You talking about this photoshoot gig?" Palmer didn't sound impressed. "Cost me a whole load of extra money, you know, hiring this hotshot photographer from New York—and chartering this catamaran too! What's the point of having the girls pose out here, when nobody can see them? Girls strutting their stuff onstage in front of a live crowd— *that's* what people want to see in a bikini contest!"

"And we'll have that," Gina reassured him. "But that's so boring and clichéd now. Every bikini contest has that. You said you wanted to stand out from the crowd, right? What we're doing here is closer to the big TV shows, like *America's Next Top Model* and other reality TV shows like that. We're giving the girls challenges so that they can compete against each other in different ways. We'll show the best photos from each girl's shoot and get people to vote for their favorite online, maybe start a fan following for some of the girls, maybe even spread some false rumors about rivalry and drama on set... People love that kind of salacious gossip and it'll get them talking about the show."

"They don't seem to be talking much yet," grumbled Palmer, although he was starting to sound mollified.

"Trust me, they will. Just give it time," said Gina confidently. "And it will be fantastic brand exposure for Bronzed Babe too. All the girls will be posing with a bottle of sunscreen in the photos, which means the public will see your products much more and the contest will promote your company much better than just having the girls strut up and down a catwalk."

"Well, OK, that's good—but why do we have to include that damn bird in the photoshoot?" Palmer complained.

Gina laughed. "You mean the parrot? I thought that was a fantastic stroke of luck, finding out the resort has a resident scarlet macaw. It looks exactly like the one on your sunscreen bottles. Come on, these photos will be like the living embodiment of your brand logo. It's perfect! And Hemingway is a great personality. He looks awesome on camera, plus..." Gina gave a throaty chuckle. "...you never know, having him involved just might stir up some of the animal rights people, get them complaining about the contest."

"Huh? Why the hell would we want that?" demanded Palmer.

"Oh, any publicity is good publicity in my book," purred Gina. "Don't worry, I've checked all the legal angles and we're covered. You're not going to get in trouble for animal cruelty or anything. But a few well-placed rumors here and there... well, there's nothing like scandal and controversy to generate publicity, especially on social media!"

"Just as long as you don't start digging for skeletons in *my* closet," warned Palmer, in a tone that was only half-joking. "OK, so you talk a good talk, Miss Ross, but you'd better not let me down. Hiring your agency is costing me an arm and a leg—we've never used a professional PR and events management outfit before. So you better show me that it's worth forking out all these extra bucks."

"Don't worry, Mr. Palmer, you'll get more than your money's worth," said Gina. "I'm known as the best in the business, because I get results—no matter what it takes."

CHAPTER THREE

Ellie waited until she heard the voices fading away and there was total silence for a few minutes before she stepped out of the en suite head. She peeked out into the companionway: it was empty. Quickly, she ran up the steps and through the saloon, until she was back on the aft deck. There, she walked casually to the guardrail and scanned the area. She could see Gina with the group of bikini contestants at the bow, together with the photographer and a few members of the crew. Don Palmer, however, was not with them. He had returned to his leather settee up on the flybridge, where he was now talking loudly on his cellphone. His voice drifted down to Ellie and she shook her head as she realized that he was bragging about the success of his bikini pageant.

What a hypocritical liar, she thought in disgust as

she remembered what she'd overheard below deck. *Still, it's none of my business anyway*, she reminded herself as she drifted down to join the group at the front of the catamaran.

Aunt Olive was watching the proceedings from a comfortable couch in the forward cockpit, but Ellie decided not to join her. Instead, she drifted over to join the group surrounding the photographer. It seemed that each girl was taking turns up on the tip of the bow, striking different poses while holding a bottle of Bronzed Babe sunscreen and smiling back at the camera. As Ellie watched, she marveled at how confident the girls were in front of the lens, thrusting out their breasts and angling their hips in such a way as to make the most of their curves. Some raised their arms gracefully above their heads; others tilted their heads coyly to let the best light capture their features. With the backdrop of the gleaming white catamaran and the sparkling blue waters of the Gulf behind them, it made for some stunning photographs.

"...beautiful... yes, yes... great... awesome... just like that!" chanted the photographer, darting left and right whilst the shutter on his camera clicked away. "Now look over at me... that's it... chin a bit higher... good... sexy, sexy... yes... I like that... awesome!" He stood up and nodded at the girl. "That's great, Destiny—you're done now."

The pretty brunette tossed her hair one last time and rose from where she had been lounging against the guardrail. She handed the bottle of sunscreen to Gina, then sashayed over to join the other girls, who were huddled together, talking and giggling. Ellie noticed that Roxy was standing at the edge of the group, looking shy.

"OK, who's next?" asked the photographer.

Gina consulted her clipboard. "We've just got Roxy and Amber and then we're done." She glanced at the sun, low in the sky. "Just as well—we're running out of time."

"Well, things would go a lot faster if you wouldn't insist on having that damn parrot in the shots," grumbled the photographer, shooting a dirty look at Hemingway the scarlet macaw, who was perched inside a cage at the side of the deck. "If it's just the girls, everything goes without a hitch, but the minute we try to get the macaw in the picture, everything gets screwed up." He wagged a finger at Gina. "You know there's a reason they say never work with children or animals."

"The bird's important," said Gina firmly. "A macaw is the mascot for the brand—it's the most recognizable part of the Bronzed Babe logo. We have to have him in some of the pictures. The ones without him are nice, but they're just like any other regular bikini shoot: no big deal."

The photographer scowled.

"I hired you because you said you can deal with anything," said Gina. "I would have thought you could figure out how to work this angle."

"You didn't tell me 'this angle' involved a huge parrot that could bite your finger off."

"Aw, come on," said Gina scornfully. "Hemingway's not dangerous—he's just a dumb bird!"

"*YOU TALKIN' TO ME?*" said Hemingway suddenly from his cage, in his best Robert De Niro voice. "*YOU TALKIN' TO ME? YOU TALKIN' TO ME?*"

Gina tried to ignore Hemingway, pretending that she hadn't heard him. She cleared her throat and continued: "They keep him around the resort like some tame pet. He's totally harmless."

"*I'M GONNA CUT YOUR HEART OUT WITH A SPOON!*" screeched Hemingway, in a perfect imitation of Alan Rickman as the Sheriff of Nottingham.

Gina flushed and Ellie had to turn away slightly to hide her smile. Some guest at the resort must have been teaching the parrot famous movie quotes, and Hemingway had obviously picked things up quickly.

"Sounds like he understands you just fine," said the photographer, grinning.

Gina scowled and gave the parrot a contemptuous look. "He's not really talking. He's just mimicking sounds he hears—he doesn't really understand the words."

"*GO AHEAD, MAKE MY DAY,*" growled Hemingway. "*I'M GONNA KICK YOUR A—*"

"Oh-kay!" cut in Gina hastily. "Uh... Roxy? Roxy, you're on next."

The girl came forward hesitantly and walked to the tip of the starboard hull. She tried to pose like Destiny had done, arranging her limbs awkwardly against the guardrail as the photographer began snapping away.

"No, no, no! For Pete's sake, don't you have any idea how to pose?" growled the photographer, glaring at Roxy. "Standing like that makes you look really fat. You need to suck your stomach in... and extend one leg to elongate them... yes... and arms away from the body... give me interesting shapes and angles... and don't pull that face... you gotta look at the lens without squinting... no, not like that! Jesus, do I have to teach Modeling 101 as well?" He gave an impatient sigh and lowered his camera to demonstrate a pose. "Like this, OK? And then shift and change the pose slightly every time I click the shutter."

Ellie felt her heart go out to Roxy as she watched the other girl. Roxy looked flushed and miserable, and only became more flustered as the photographer kept barking instructions. Although she tried to copy what the other girls had been doing, her lack of confidence really showed, making her look stiff and awkward. And when they brought Hemingway out of his cage, it only made things worse. Instead of interacting with Roxy, like he'd done with the other girls, the macaw perched on the guardrail with his back to her and refused to look at her.

The photographer swore. "What is that damn bird

doing? He looks like he's giving her the cold shoulder! How's that gonna look good in the photos?"

"Hemingway! Woohoo! Hemingway!" Gina called, waving her arms. "Look this way!"

The parrot pointedly ignored her.

"Well, don't just stand there—do something!" said the photographer, rolling his eyes at Roxy. "Try to get the bird to interact with you!"

Roxy hesitated, then held out a tentative hand toward the parrot. "Uh... hello, Hemingway?"

"*NASTY BROCCOLI!*" screeched the macaw.

Then he lunged at Roxy with his beak. She cried out and jerked her hand back just in time. The other girls screamed and everyone rushed forward.

"Are you OK?"

"What happened? Did he bite you?"

"Omigod—"

"I'm... I'm OK," said Roxy shakily.

The photographer whistled. "Man, that bird is a psycho! What's all that stuff about broccoli?"

"He hates broccoli," the resort staff member who had accompanied Hemingway on the trip spoke up. "The vet told us that we need to feed Hemingway more dark green vegetables, but he always picks the broccoli out of his food dish and throws it at people he doesn't like. It got so bad with guests getting hit in the face with broccoli that we gave up trying to feed it to him."

Roxy gave Gina a pleading look. "Can I do my shots without the parrot?"

Gina pressed her lips together. "Get some food that he *does* like," she said, not answering the girl's question. "Animals are always doing tricks for treats, right?" She glanced at a member of the crew. "You got anything he really likes to eat?"

"Hemingway loves spicy nuts," Ellie blurted out. "Especially the resort's own house mix. Have you got any of that?"

"Yeah, I think we've got some in the galley. I'll go look," offered the crew member.

He returned a few minutes later with a bag of mixed nuts and was about to hand them over to Gina when the photographer stopped him.

"No, give them to her," he said, pointing at Ellie. "You saw how the bird responded to her voice?"

It was true: Hemingway had turned around when Ellie spoke up, and he looked curious and engaged for the first time since being taken out of his cage. He cocked his head and ruffled his feathers, eyeing Ellie with anticipation.

"That's perfect!" said the photographer, adding to Roxy, "Quick—get closer to the bird and strike a pose!"

Roxy shuffled nearer Hemingway and put a hand awkwardly on her hip. The photographer jerked his head at Ellie. "Keep talking to the parrot! Keep him looking this way!"

Ellie hesitated, glancing at Gina, who shrugged and handed her the bag of nuts. Feeling embarrassed with everyone's eyes on her, Ellie stepped directly behind the photographer. She lifted the bag and shook it, making the nuts rattle inside.

"Hemingway!" she cooed. "Look! Your favorite... Wanna nut?" she said, using one of his favorite phrases.

The parrot's pupils dilated, and he spread his wings out, screeching excitedly: "WANNA NUT? WANNA NUT?"

"Yeah! That looks awesome! Keep it up... keep it up!" the photographer urged, snapping away with his camera. Roxy seemed to have relaxed slightly as well, now that the spotlight was no longer on her, and managed to strike a few good poses.

"That's it... that's it... *Got it!*" The photographer straightened at last with satisfaction.

Roxy breathed a sigh of relief and went to rejoin the other girls. The photographer turned to Ellie, who was rewarding Hemingway with a large Brazil nut, and said:

"Good work. You're the first person that bird has responded to all afternoon. You got any experience wrangling animals?"

Ellie laughed. "Oh no, not at all! I think it's just that I've built up a relationship with Hemingway in the past few weeks."

"We could use that," said the photographer. "It would make things go a lot smoother—"

"Oh, Ellie can help out with the last shoot," said Gina quickly.

Ellie felt slightly annoyed that Gina hadn't

bothered to ask her, she'd just assumed—but she nodded and said, "Of course. I'm happy to help."

Amber, the last contestant to be photographed, sashayed forward. Ellie looked enviously again at the girl's svelte figure and thick auburn hair, which fell in waves down her back. But it wasn't so much her looks which made her so eye-catching; it was her self-assurance. Amber oozed confidence, and the difference between her and Roxy was glaring.

"Where do you want me?" she drawled, pausing with one hand on a hip. It should have been an affected pose, but somehow Amber made it look natural and sexy.

"Hmm... we haven't done any shots on the trampoline for a while," said the photographer. "Let's have you in the middle for a couple of shots, and then maybe we can have some with you and the parrot by the crossbeam?"

Amber lowered herself onto the trampoline, which was stretched across the empty space between the two bows of the catamaran, and took up a position against the far edge of the mesh fabric. She obviously loved being in front of the camera and had no problem striking several provocative poses, arching her back and stretching her legs out.

"Beautiful! Beautiful... yeah, just like that! You're a natural," crowed the photographer. "OK, how about some action shots—try to get some movement into the pictures, huh?"

Amber obligingly stood up and began bouncing on

the trampoline, curving her body this way and that, and throwing the camera coy looks as she rose and fell in the air.

"Oh... awesome! Awesome!" cried the photographer, snapping manically away.

Amber grinned at him and bounced higher and higher. She laughed and tossed her head back, her beautiful auburn hair fanning out around her head like a cloud. Then, as she bounced once more and came down on the trampoline, there came a horrible ripping sound.

Amber screamed as her legs plunged suddenly through a hole that had torn open in the trampoline fabric. Her whole body fell in and, the next moment, she was dangling above the rushing water with only her head and arms above the hole.

She screamed and clawed desperately at the edges of the trampoline. Her struggling only caused the fabric to tear away from the fastenings even more. Several people rushed forward but they hesitated at the edge of the trampoline, worried that if they put their weight on the fabric, the strain would cause the hole to widen.

"Help!" cried Amber, the whites of her eyes showing. "Hel—"

The rest of her cry was torn away as she suddenly lost her grip. With a terrified scream, she slipped through the hole and plunged into the ocean.

CHAPTER FOUR

"Oh my God!"

"*Amber!*"

"MAN OVERBOARD!"

There was a flurry of activity on deck as the catamaran crew rushed into action. The bikini contest girls rushed to the side of the catamaran and anxiously scanned the ocean for any signs of Amber. Ellie joined them, thinking uneasily of the churning water that Amber had fallen into. She would have been trapped beneath the catamaran, close to the propellers... could she have escaped without injury?

Then suddenly someone squealed and someone else yelled: "I see her! There she is!"

Ellie breathed a sigh of relief as she saw Amber's head break the surface a short distance from the boat. The girl shook the water out of her eyes and treaded water, looking around. She spotted the boat and waved, signaling that she was all right. Her red hair had darkened from being wet and was now plastered to her head, making her look like a sleek, brown seal. She moved like a seal too, cutting fluidly through the water as she began swimming toward the catamaran with strong, clean strokes. As someone who had only just recently learned how to swim, Ellie watched Amber's technique with admiration.

One of the crew had thrown out a life ring and a rescue line, and Amber grabbed these as the catamaran was carefully maneuvered alongside her. A few minutes later, she was being hauled, breathless and dripping, back on board via the transom at the stern. People hovered around, wrapping her in towels, offering hot drinks, and generally fussing over her. The other bikini contest girls surrounded her, goggle-eyed, as Amber recounted her ordeal in dramatic detail. Luckily, she had managed to escape injury during her fall, and her strong swimming ability meant that even her unexpected dip in the ocean hadn't really affected her composure. In fact, she looked like she was enjoying all the attention and was reveling in her new role as "heroine of the hour."

"What the hell happened?" demanded Don Palmer, having come down from the flybridge when he heard the commotion.

"There was an accident; the trampoline ripped—"

"What?" Palmer turned angrily to the catamaran skipper. "You promised me the highest standards of safety on this boat. How did this happen?"

The captain shook his head in bewilderment. "I don't understand it. There's no reason for the trampoline to break."

"It could just be wear and tear," one of the bikini contestants spoke up. "My dad's got a catamaran. It's a lot smaller than this, but he says you gotta check the mesh fabric regularly."

"But it *was* checked!" said the captain. "In fact, the old trampoline was replaced with this new one just a few weeks ago. There's just no reason for it to rip."

Suddenly, there was a shout from the bow of the catamaran and, when everyone turned to look, they found one of the crew members kneeling by the edge of the torn trampoline.

"It looks like some of the stitches around the side have been cut!" he called out.

"*What?*"

There were gasps and cries of horror from the girls.

"Omigod, you mean someone deliberately sabotaged the trampoline?" asked Destiny.

"Any one of us could have been on it when it ripped away," cried Kimberley.

"We could have been killed!"

"It's the hex," said Roxy with a scared look.

"Yeah, someone is out to get us!"

"Maybe a serial killer!"

"*I SEE DEAD PEOPLE!*" screeched Hemingway from his cage.

Gina's cool voice cut through the hubbub. "There's no hex or serial killer or anything. Accidents happen all the time, even when things are checked—that's why they're called accidents, right?" she said brightly. "But no one got hurt so we're all good, OK? Now, why don't we all go into the saloon and get some nice, long drinks while the captain turns us around to head back to shore."

The girls subsided and began milling down the deck, towards the entrance to the saloon. Ellie could still hear whispers being exchanged, though, and she didn't blame them. Despite Gina's best efforts, it seemed clear that what had happened had been no "accident"—the trampoline had been deliberately tampered with. For the rest of the journey, despite the balmy weather, smooth conditions, and gorgeous views, the girls remained huddled together in the saloon. There seemed to be an audible sigh of relief when the catamaran pulled into the marina at last. It was a sober party that finally disembarked from the shuttle bus which took them back to the Sunset Palms Beach Resort.

Ellie let the others get off the bus first and sat in her seat for a moment, looking out at the front façade of the main resort building. She felt a rush of fondness as she took in the familiar red carpet leading up to the front door, the smiling bellmen waiting to help with luggage, the large swinging colonial-style doors, and the potted palms flanking the entrance. An unexpected sense of homecoming surprised her. Although she had only been staying at the Sunset Palms Beach Resort for a few weeks now, it was starting to feel a bit like "home."

Or at least a home away from home, thought Ellie with a smile. It was an odd thing to feel about a vacation resort, but perhaps it was because so much had happened since she'd arrived in Florida. The resort had become so much more than just a place to sleep and eat and lounge by the pool. There were friends she had made, beautiful secluded corners of the grounds she'd discovered, new skills she had learned, and experiences she had relished—not to mention the permanent residents she'd fallen in love with, like Hemingway the macaw and Mojito the resort cat... *And maybe a handsome doctor too?* added an insidious little voice in her head.

Hastily, Ellie pushed the thought away. She grabbed her things and followed the rest of the group off the bus. She was pleased to see that the return to the familiar surroundings of the resort seemed to have restored the girls' good spirits. They were chatting and laughing in a more normal manner now as they followed Gina in through the front entrance. But they had barely started making their way across the wide lobby when a middle-aged woman with long hair streaked with grey suddenly sprang up from the seating area and ran toward them.

She whipped a homemade cardboard placard out of a large beach bag and started waving it, chanting: "Beauty is not skin-deep! All women are beautiful—don't be enslaved by men's pathetic obsessions!"

She turned to two of the girls, who shrank away from her, and thrust herself in their faces, demanding: "Why are you doing this? Why are you being part of this degrading myth that a woman's main purpose in life is just to be attractive?"

Without waiting for them to answer, she whirled toward a couple of other girls and shook her fist at them. "Don't you know that bikini contests put tremendous pressure on women to conform to stupid beauty standards? They force you to go on extreme diets and deprive yourself of water and nutrients, just to get a lame title based on how little fat and how much spray tan you have on!"

"No one is forcing anyone to do anything," cut in Gina sharply, trying to step between the woman and the bikini contestants. "These girls are here of their own free will and they're proud to take part in one of the most prestigious events in the Tampa Bay calendar—"

"Prestigious event, my ass!" snapped the woman. "This is nothing more than a cattle auction! Yes, that's right! These girls are just like meat being displayed at a butcher, while men eyeball their boobs and slobber over them. It's disgusting!" She turned and jabbed an accusing finger at Don Palmer, who was bringing up the rear of the group. "And you're no better than a pimp!"

"Hey! Who're you calling a pimp?" demanded Palmer angrily.

"I'll call you more than that, you no-good son of a bi—"

"You can't talk to me like that!" growled Palmer, his face going red.

"I'll talk to you any way I want," said the woman, thrusting her chin out aggressively. "I'm not scared of you! I know all your dirty little secrets and you can't buy me off. I know about you and the—"

"SECURITY!" bellowed Palmer. "Get this old witch out of here!"

The resort security guards, as well as various bellmen and reception staff, had already been congregating at the first sound of raised voices, and now they rushed forward. But when they tried to approach the woman, she began to shriek and shout even louder.

"Bullies! Toads!" she screamed. "Misogynistic pigs!"

Her screaming set Hemingway off and he started screeching as well, flapping his wings in his cage and causing even more chaos. The din in the lobby became deafening. People turned and stared, while the resort staff hovered around the woman, as if unsure how to deal with her. The security guards tried to take hold of her arms, but she struggled furiously and screamed even louder, accusing them of abuse and oppression.

"Get Mr. Papadopoulos," someone said urgently.

"He's not here today!"

"Then get the doc!"

Ellie's heart skipped a beat as, a few minutes later, a handsome young man entered the lobby from the rear doors and pushed his way through the crowd. With his tall, athletic figure, warm brown eyes, and beach-surfer good looks, it was easy to see why Dr. Blake Thornton was the resort's unofficial heartthrob. Right now, though, it was his air of cool command that made people look to him with relief. He approached the woman and the guards parted to let him through. She turned defiantly to face him, her eyes flashing, then faltered slightly as she took in his calm demeanor.

"What... what d'you want? Come to arrest me, huh?" she said, trying to maintain her belligerence in the face of Blake's quiet authority.

"I'm a doctor, not a policeman," said Blake mildly. "But I *am* responsible for guests' wellbeing at the resort and—"

"Well, I'm a guest at the resort too," said the woman quickly. "I have just as much right to be here as anyone else!"

"Yes, but you don't have the right to harass the other guests," replied Blake, his tone polite but with a firm edge. "I'm sorry, ma'am, but if you cannot control yourself and refrain from attacking others, whether verbally or physically, then I will have to ask the guards to remove you from the premises."

"You... you can't stop me speaking the truth!" cried the woman. "I have a duty to expose the filthy reality of this shameful contest!"

"Well, how about if we discuss that in my office?" suggested Blake, still calm and patient.

"Yes, brilliant idea... and with a nice cup of tea!"

Ellie turned in surprise as Aunt Olive sallied forth suddenly. She went up and linked arms with the woman, beaming at her.

"So nice to meet a fellow Second Wave Feminist! I didn't realize there was any of the sisterhood here at the resort. So, what have you done?" she asked chattily, as if asking about the woman's past vacation experiences. "Mass marches? Flour bombs? Stealth flyer campaigns?"

"Uh..." The woman stared at Aunt Olive, temporarily speechless.

"I like chucking tomatoes best," continued Aunt Olive in a confidential tone. "Although I do wish I had been old enough to go to the Miss America protest. I would have loved to do some bra-burning—"

"That's a myth! There was never any bra-burning," protested the woman. "They just like to use that image to make fun of feminists, but they never burned any bras! Mostly, they just threw high heels and lipsticks and other symbols of oppression into the 'Freedom Trashcan.' A couple of girls threw in some underwear but there was no fire."

"Oh, well, I would have loved to have burned my bra," said Aunt Olive, undaunted. "Especially the underwired ones—don't you just hate those? I *have* managed to find some push-up bras which don't use wire, though." She leaned close and said in a loud stage whisper: "The trick is in having thick straps and four-way stretch, not to mention full-cup padding. But you've got to be careful to lift and separate, to avoid 'mono-boob.' Of course, they do say we shouldn't be worrying about such things at our age, but I say—why shouldn't I have perky breasts in my sixties?"

By now, the woman was standing with her mouth open and a glazed look in her eyes. In fact, the whole lobby seemed to have been stunned into silence, listening to Aunt Olive warble on about "mono-boobs" and "perky breasts." Ellie bit back a laugh and shook her head in admiration as her aunt gently took the woman's elbow a few minutes later and began steering her toward the rear lobby doors. The woman went docilely, without another word of protest, while Blake followed them, looking bemused. The rest of the lobby gave a collective sigh of relief and the normal hum of activity and conversation slowly resumed.

The last thing Ellie saw was Aunt Olive glancing back to give her a wink, before leading the woman out into the sunshine.

CHAPTER FIVE

When Ellie arrived at the resort's breakfast buffet the next morning, the first thing she saw was Gina and the group of bikini contestants sitting at a large table on the outdoor deck. All the girls were chattering happily to each other and seemed to have forgotten about the frightening events of the previous day. All except Roxy, who sat quietly between the other girls and sipped her coffee. Her face lit up, though, when she saw Ellie, and she waved eagerly.

"You go and join them, dear," said Aunt Olive as Ellie hesitated. "I'm going to sit with Sandy."

"Who?" said Ellie, then her eyes widened as she saw who her aunt was pointing to: the woman who had caused the commotion in the lobby the day before. "You're going to sit with *her*?"

"Yes, why not?"

Ellie eyed the woman's wild grey hair, baggy clothes, and boho-style headscarf, and pulled a face. "She's one of those loony feminists, isn't she? Always yelling and protesting about things."

Aunt Olive glowered at her. "Women like Sandy O'Brien are the reason that you can vote and use contraception and have a career nowadays, young lady."

Ellie ducked her head in apology. "Yes, I know, but... why do you want to *socialize* with her? Isn't she... well, a troublemaker?"

Aunt Olive chuckled. "That would be reason enough! I'm a troublemaker too, poppet, in case you haven't noticed," she said with a wink. "Anyway, I like Sandy. She might be a bit aggressive in her methods, but she means well. And she's led a fascinating life. I can't wait to hear more about it." She narrowed her eyes thoughtfully. "In fact, I've got an idea for a new book and she would be the *perfect* inspiration for the heroine..."

Still muttering to herself, Aunt Olive left Ellie and made her way across to Sandy O'Brien's table. Ellie went to join the bikini contestants and slid into an empty chair just as Gina stood up and made some kind of announcement. Ellie didn't hear what it was, but she was surprised by the sudden whooping and cheering.

"What's all the excitement about?" she asked Roxy across the table.

"Oh, Gina just told us that the owner of the resort

has given us all a free spa day, just to help us chill out and recover from what happened yesterday! Isn't that awesome of him?" said Roxy.

"Yes, Mr. Papadopoulos is the loveliest man," Ellie agreed, smiling.

"It's great because it'll help us relax for the day after tomorrow. That's our big day," Roxy explained, seeing Ellie's puzzled look. "It's the finale: we'll have to walk the catwalk in front of a live audience and stand together on stage."

"Oh, yes! I saw them erecting the stage on one of the lawns, when my aunt and I walked over from our villa just now," said Ellie. "There were posters all over the lobby and around the pool as well, advertising the event."

Roxy nodded, adding nervously, "I hope I do OK. I've never had to walk a catwalk before. I'm so scared I'll trip and embarrass myself or something!"

"I'm sure you'll be fine," Ellie reassured her. "Why don't you ask the other girls for help? Who's your roommate? I'm sure she'd be happy to give you some tips."

Roxy looked even more uncertain. "That's Amber and I'm too scared of her to ask her anything! She's, like, really popular and really confident." She sighed. "Sometimes I wonder why I came. I just don't fit in with the other girls, and anyway, it's not like I have any real chance of winning. I mean, it's obvious that either Brandi or Amber are going to get the title."

Ellie looked down the table once more and

couldn't help silently agreeing. The two girls in question were undeniably the most attractive—and not just because of their looks and perfect hourglass figures. All the girls in the contest were pretty, but Amber and Brandi overshadowed them with their confidence and vivacious personalities. They were also bitter rivals, judging by the narrow-eyed looks they were giving each other across the table.

"If they don't kill each other first," Ellie said jokingly.

Roxy giggled. "Yeah, they're, like, ultra-competitive all the time and really jealous of each other. They're both so gorgeous, though; I don't know how the judges are going to choose."

Then Ellie was distracted by hearing her own name being called and she looked up in surprise to find Gina speaking to her:

"Ellie—Mr. Papadopoulos included you in the invitation too," said Gina coolly. "He heard about the way you helped out with Hemingway on the catamaran yesterday and said you deserved a treat too, as an unofficial member of the team."

"Oh!" said Ellie, surprised and pleased. "That's really sweet and generous of him!"

Gina gave a tight smile. "Yes, you can come straight to the spa with us after breakfast. The treatments are booked for ten o'clock."

So Ellie found herself accompanying the bikini contestants to the resort spa later that morning. Stepping into the serene courtyard surrounding the front entrance—with its gurgling water features and lush tropical plantings—instantly gave Ellie a sense of calm, and this was enhanced as they entered the spa itself. The interior was decorated in bamboo and natural fabrics, in soft shades of cream and aquamarine, and the staff wore matching uniforms. Mood music featuring the sound of ocean waves played from hidden speakers and the air was filled with the soothing fragrance of lavender.

A smiling receptionist greeted them and handed out menus with the spa's treatments.

"You've got the whole spa to yourselves this morning," she said brightly. "So you can have anything you like, although I highly recommend our signature facial. It's our most popular treatment and it includes an amazing mask which has collagen-boosting properties. You'll leave with awesome skin that's glowing and hydrated!"

"I'm gonna have that," declared Brandi.

"Me too," said Amber quickly.

The other girls echoed them—all except Roxy who asked hesitantly:

"Uh... can I have something else instead? I... I don't like facials."

Ellie glanced at Roxy, noting that she had reapplied the same thick make-up she'd worn the previous day, even though most of the other girls had come barefaced to the spa. It seemed that Roxy was so shy and insecure, she needed her heavy make-up as a form of emotional crutch. Ellie felt her heart go out to the girl and wished that she could reassure Roxy that she had no need to be so self-conscious. *Self-esteem is such a funny thing*, she thought. It was like all the Hollywood actresses or music stars who were sensitive about their alleged big noses or high foreheads or small eyes, when all the world saw were gorgeous women with perfect features.

"Oh, sure," said the receptionist, smiling at Roxy. "How about an herbal soak? That's basically a spa bath with essential oils and herbs. The aromatic steam is really good for you and the hot water helps to open your pores and activate the oils, so they can penetrate deeper." Seeing Roxy's lack of enthusiasm, she added, "Or you could pick from any of our massages. Or have a mani or a pedi—"

"Oh yes, a pedicure," said Roxy. She looked down at her toes. "It'll be good to get my nails refreshed before the finale."

"I won't have a treatment either. I'll just go to the steam room and relax—just what I need after all the long hours I've been working lately," said Gina, wriggling her shoulders. She glanced at Ellie, then added, "But I think Ellie would like the pedicure too."

Ellie felt a flash of annoyance at Gina's bossy attitude. "No, I think I'll go for the signature facial as well," she said firmly.

"Great! Now, if you'll just come this way, ladies…" The receptionist led them around the corner to a long corridor with five doors opening off on each side. "You'll each be in one of these rooms. There's a ladies' changing room at the end of the corridor. You'll find terrycloth robes in there for you to put on. There are also wall cubicles with baskets for you to leave your personal belongings. We don't have lockers here so we normally ask guests to leave their valuables in their rooms, but if you have any jewelry or other items that you're worried about, please leave them with me at the reception."

The receptionist paused, then added, "Oh yes— before I forget. The other door at the end is the restroom. We had a sudden leak this morning and there's a large puddle all over the floor. The resort plumber is on his way but, until then, you'll find the floor quite wet if you have to use the restroom, so please be careful."

She turned to indicate a group of smiling women wearing identical spa uniforms, who had appeared behind her. "These are the beauticians who'll be looking after you today. They'll be waiting out here for you when you've changed into your robes to show you to your rooms."

Ellie followed the other girls into the changing room, feeling almost like she was on a school trip. There was lots of chatter, teasing, and giggling as they all undressed and got into the fluffy terrycloth bathrobes. Ellie noticed, though, that there was a distinct coolness between Amber and Brandi, with the two of them exchanging snide remarks and even openly catty insults about each other's appearance, just like they had on the catamaran.

So much for the 'great sisterhood' talked about in all the PR, thought Ellie wryly. She recalled what Gina had said yesterday to Sandy O'Brien about the contest fostering bonds of womanhood and female camaraderie. For some of the girls, at least, the rivalry was very real and very vicious.

CHAPTER SIX

Ellie followed the other girls back out into the corridor where the spa's beauty therapists were waiting to direct them to their rooms. She waited as Amber and Brandi were given the first two rooms on one side, before she was assigned to the third, and she noted the door to the steam room was directly opposite hers on the other side of the corridor. The rest of the girls were shown to the remaining rooms and there was a lot of giggling and milling about as some of the girls went into the wrong rooms by mistake.

Once she was settled in her own room, Ellie was impressed by how good the soundproofing was: with her door shut, she couldn't hear the other girls at all. Any faint sounds were muffled by the soothing music from the central speakers. She could almost have imagined that she was alone at the spa.

"Have you had a facial before?" asked the smiling beautician.

"Yes, but not for ages," said Ellie, adding with a grin: "And it wasn't in such a luxurious spa, in such beautiful surroundings." She gestured round the room, softly lit by scented candles, and at the French doors at one end which looked out on a narrow strip of the spa garden. Beyond the dense greenery, she could see the brushwood fencing surrounding the garden, and beyond that, a glimpse of the vivid blue sky.

The beautician followed her gaze out of the French doors. "Yeah, this is the nicest spa I've worked at. And you're lucky—the treatment rooms on this side of the corridor all have windows looking out into the garden. I always try to get a room on this side when I make a booking; it means I'm not stuck indoors all day with no natural light when I'm working my shift. Oh, but don't worry about privacy," she added quickly. "They've made sure that the sides of the spa garden are off limits to the public, so no one can wander around by mistake and spy on clients in the treatment rooms."

Not that they can see much anyway, with so many plants out there, thought Ellie, looking again at the lush ferns and other tropical plants growing right outside the French doors.

She sat down in one of the deep armchairs by the French doors, as the beautician placed a footbath by her feet.

"Ooh... this feels wonderful," said Ellie in surprise as she plunged her bare feet into the warm, fragrant water. "I thought it would be weird to soak in hot water on a sunny day, but it actually feels really lovely."

"Oh yes, warm water always relaxes the muscles much better than anything else," said the beautician.

Ellie leaned back and relished the feeling of the soothing warmth from the footbath traveling up her legs and into her whole body. The beautician began to give her a foot massage and, by the time she finished, Ellie felt like she had melted into the armchair. She could barely find the strength to pull herself up and climb onto the treatment bed in the center of the room. She sighed with pleasure as she stretched out on the soft terrycloth cover. The beautician covered her with a fluffy towel that had been on a heated rail and Ellie felt like she was being wrapped up in a warm cocoon.

Closing her eyes, she sighed again and smiled to herself. *Mmm... this is what being on vacation is all about*, she thought dreamily. She sensed the beautician leaning over her, peering at her face, and wondered fleetingly if the beautician was horrified by the state of her skin.

She'll probably tell me I should be moisturizing more... and using sunscreen more regularly... and exfoliating once a week, mused Ellie. *Maybe she'll have some good tips for how to deal with my freckles…*

She half expected to feel gentle fingers on her face but, to her surprise, she heard the beautician murmur: "Sorry… I just need to go get something… I'll be right back"—and the next moment, there was the sound of the woman leaving the room and the door closing quietly behind her.

Ellie snuggled deeper under the fluffy towel, listening to the soothing wave sound effects mixed into the spa music. There was a soft creak and the rattle of a window, then she heard the cries of the seagulls joining the sound of the waves, as well as the loud swaying and rustling of palm trees. The rustling got louder, sounding like it was coming from the bushes right outside the French door. *Wow, talk about a realistic ambient soundtrack. I almost feel like if I opened my eyes, I'd find myself on the beach,* thought Ellie drowsily.

She was almost drifting off to sleep when she was suddenly jolted awake. Her right arm had slid down and was hanging over the side of the bed, and something cold and moist was touching her fingertips. Ellie jerked her hand up reflexively, then she raised herself up on an elbow and leaned curiously over the side of the bed. She found herself looking down at a little black whiskered face with big green eyes.

Ellie let out a sigh of exasperation. "Mojito! What are you doing here?"

"*MIAOW!*"

"I'm sure you're not supposed to be here," said Ellie, frowning.

The cat ignored her. Instead, she jumped up onto the bed, padded across the fluffy towel, and began making herself comfortable between Ellie's knees. As the resort's resident feline, Mojito was obviously used to going where she liked and the spa was no exception!

Ellie looked around, puzzled at how the cat had gotten into the room. Then she saw the answer: one of the French doors was slightly ajar. That was how Mojito had come in! No wonder she had thought that the ambient soundtrack was suddenly very realistic, with additional seagull cries and palm trees rustling... because those sounds were real!

She looked back down at the black cat, who was now happily kneading the fluffy towel. Loud purring filled the room. Ellie knew she should put Mojito back outside, but the cat looked so sweet that she didn't have the heart to move her.

"You're a little minx, you know that?" said Ellie with a mixture of fondness and exasperation.

Mojito rolled over to expose her belly and tilted her head, her green eyes big and adorable.

Ellie chuckled. "Don't try those cute eyes on me. I'm not—"

She broke off as, all of a sudden, Mojito jerked upright. The cat froze and stared at the wall between their room and Brandi's room next door. The fur on her back raised into hackles and she hissed.

"Mojito? What is it?" asked Ellie, surprised.

The cat hissed again, her gaze still riveted on the wall. Her ears flicked and swiveled from side to side, as if she were listening to something. Ellie turned her own gaze to stare at the wall, straining to hear any noises coming through the partition, but she could hear nothing above the rhythmic music of the ocean waves still playing from the speakers.

The cat had clearly heard something, though. She was standing up now, her back stiff and arched, and her tail whipping from side to side while she continued to stare at the wall. Obviously, the animal's superior sense of hearing could detect sounds well beyond the human ear. Ellie told herself not to be silly, but Mojito's strange behavior was making her uneasy.

Finally, she got up and slid off the bed with a sigh. There was no way she was going to be able to go back to her previous relaxed state now. She wondered where her beautician was and wished she would come back, so that she could help to remove the cat.

Wait—I can do it myself, thought Ellie. *All I need to do is chuck Mojito back out into the spa garden through the French doors.*

Turning back to the bed, she bent to scoop up the little feline, but Mojito was too quick for her. She darted out of Ellie's reach and jumped off the bed, scampering across to the cabinets lining the wall.

"Mojito! Come here!" hissed Ellie.

"*MIAOW!*" said the cat cheekily, pawing at one of

the cabinet doors. It was obviously a trick she had done many times before, because she deftly caught the edge with her claws and pulled, swinging the door open. A second later, she had slipped inside the cabinet, disappearing from sight.

"Ooh! Mojito!" Ellie fumed.

She bent down to look through the open cabinet door. The space inside seemed to be crammed with all sorts of spa supplies and accessories. Ellie crouched lower to look deeper into the cabinet and saw two glowing green eyes peering back out at her from behind a big bag of cotton balls.

"Mojito! Come out here!" she demanded.

"*MIAOW!*" came the defiant reply.

Ellie sighed and reached into the cabinet to grab hold of the cat. Her fingers groped and found a sleek, furry body but, the next moment, Mojito wriggled past her hands and shot out of the cabinet. She ran past Ellie and made for the door of the room, which wasn't quite closed. Once again, Mojito caught the edge of the door with her paw and pulled it open, then she slipped into the corridor outside.

Great, thought Ellie with annoyance. *Now she's loose in the spa!*

For a moment, she was half tempted to just push her room door shut and climb back onto the bed. Ignore the whole thing. After all, it wasn't really her problem. Mojito was the resort cat and she was sure the spa staff were used to dealing with the naughty feline's antics.

But something made Ellie hesitate. Maybe it was a sense of responsibility she felt, since Mojito had come in through *her* window. After all, she should probably have grabbed the cat as soon as Mojito had jumped on the bed and immediately put the animal back outside. Her own slow response and indulgent attitude had contributed to the present situation. Or maybe it was because she still felt faintly disturbed by Mojito's strange behavior. Whatever it was, Ellie grabbed her bathrobe and made the decision to go after the cat.

As she stepped out into the corridor, she caught a glimpse of Gina in her terrycloth robe just entering the steam room opposite and the door shutting quietly after her. Ellie glanced quickly up and down the corridor, but it was empty.

Where is that cat? she thought. Then she noticed that the door at the bottom of the corridor was slightly open. It was the one that the receptionist had pointed out as the ladies' restroom. Maybe Mojito had gone in there?

Pulling her bathrobe tighter around her, Ellie hurried down to the bottom of the corridor. She pushed the swinging door open and stepped inside, then exclaimed in annoyance as she stepped into a huge puddle.

"Ugh!"

Too late, she remembered what the receptionist had said about the leak. She could see now that the entire floor was flooded and there was a little yellow plastic "hazard" sign placed in the middle to warn clients.

They should really put it outside the door, thought Ellie grumpily. *What's the point when you've stepped inside already and got your feet wet?*

Anyway, it was obvious that Mojito wasn't in here, so she retreated into the corridor and tracked wet footprints all the way back to her room. At her door, she hesitated, wondering whether to just give up. Then she heard a faint miaowing.

"Mojito? Mojito, where are you?" she called softly.

The cat miaowed again. The cries seemed to be coming from the room next to hers. *Brandi's room*, Ellie recalled. She went up to the door and put her ear against the wood. She could hear Mojito's muffled cries inside, but no voices. *What are Brandi and her beauty therapist doing?* she wondered.

Tentatively, she knocked on the door. No response. She was just about to try again when a voice behind her said:

"Can I help you?"

Ellie turned to see a woman in a spa uniform standing behind her. She had a name badge which said: "*Monica.*"

"Oh! Hi... I was just... erm, you know Mojito the resort cat? She's got in the spa and she seems to have run into this room." She looked at the other woman quizzically. "Are you Brandi's therapist? I thought you'd be inside. That's why I was knocking."

"Oh, I ran out of some supplies so I went to the

store cupboard," Monica explained. "But Miss Harris is in there. Hasn't she answered?" As she was talking, she stepped past Ellie, pushed the door open, and went in.

Ellie followed her into the room. It looked very similar to her own, with almost identical furnishings and a counter along one wall displaying creams, lotions, and glass dispenser jars, next to a sink and stacks of folded towels.

Then Ellie noticed Mojito standing beside the bed with all her hackles raised again. Brandi was lying on the bed, just like Ellie had been, covered in a large fluffy towel, and she seemed to be fast asleep. The top of her head was pointing toward the door, so Ellie couldn't see her face, but she could see the girl's arm flung out sideways and hanging down the side of the bed.

"Miss Harris?" said Monica, walking slowly forward. Then she gave a scream and clasped a hand to her mouth, her eyes wide with horror.

Ellie rushed to her side and stared down at the bed. Brandi lay with her eyes open, staring sightlessly up at the ceiling with her mouth pulled wide, as if in a silent scream.

"Oh... oh my God..." gasped Monica. "She's dead... SHE'S DEAD!"

CHAPTER SEVEN

"It's ridiculous for the police to think that Sandy could have murdered that poor girl—absolutely ridiculous!" Aunt Olive fumed.

Ellie sat watching her aunt pace backwards and forwards across the living area of their shared villa suite. It was hard to believe that only that morning, she had been chilling out at the spa, enjoying the relaxing ambience and looking forward to several hours of pampering. As it was, she had ended up spending most of the morning answering police questions, after watching in horror as resort security and police swarmed the spa and an ME came to remove Brandi's lifeless body.

"The police are utter nincompoops! I don't know where they're getting their ideas from," seethed Aunt Olive, whirling on the spot and pacing back across the room.

"Sandy *did* attack the bikini contestants yesterday when we arrived back at the resort," Ellie pointed out.

Aunt Olive scowled. "She didn't 'attack' them—anyone would think that she went after the girls with a machete, the way you describe it! She simply staged a protest with a placard. That's hardly a vicious crime."

"Yes, but she does have a history of assault, doesn't she?" said Ellie. "That's what Detective Carson told me. He said that Sandy O'Brien had a record and she had been arrested at past protest marches for violent behavior."

"I hardly call throwing eggs at a few officers 'violent behavior,'" scoffed Aunt Olive. "I've done far worse in my youth. Sandy is passionate about women's rights and she's not afraid to take a stand. Well, good on her!"

"Yes, but perhaps she got carried away—"

"Oh fiddle-faddle! Besides, even if Sandy *had* got a bit carried away, it's ludicrous to think that she would harm one of the girls. I mean, they are the very reason she's protesting against the bikini contest! She's trying to protect them—why on earth would she want to kill one of them? If she had wanted to hurt anyone, it would have more than likely been Don Palmer. He's the owner and sponsor of the contest, and he represents everything Sandy hates about rich, arrogant men who abuse their power."

Ellie was silent. She had to admit that what her

aunt said made a lot of sense. Still, she could also see why the police had jumped on Sandy, especially given what the girls had found tucked amongst their belongings when they'd finally returned to the changing room that morning.

"It's not just her record that's making the police focus on her—it's the fact that we all found *this* stuffed in with our things," said Ellie, holding up a homemade flyer and waving it to catch her aunt's attention. "It's full of stuff about how evil beauty pageants are and how they degrade women—"

"So?"

"So that's exactly the sort of thing that Sandy was shouting in the lobby yesterday."

Aunt Olive gave a disdainful sniff. "That doesn't mean that Sandy put *those* leaflets in your bags."

"Aww, come on! You know it's more than likely that it was her. It's just too much of a coincidence to think that there would be another feminist activist running around the resort, also stalking the bikini contest girls," said Ellie. "And that means that Sandy must have sneaked into the spa this morning—which puts her at the crime scene! She doesn't have an alibi for that time, does she?"

"N-no," Aunt Olive admitted. "We parted after breakfast. I wanted to come back here to make some notes for my new book, and Sandy said she was going for a walk on the beach to hunt for seashells."

"Yes, that's what she told the police, but they couldn't find anyone who could remember seeing her."

"That doesn't mean anything," said Aunt Olive scornfully. "It's a big resort and an even bigger beach, which is shared with other resorts along this strip. There are so many people out and about, most guests wouldn't take much notice of strangers, much less remember them. They could have walked past her and never remembered. Especially as Sandy is an older woman—you know how people never notice them. They think we're just part of the background." She heaved an impatient sigh. "Besides, I keep coming back to the same thing: motive! Why on earth would Sandy want to harm Brandi? Her gripe was with the bikini contest organizers—specifically Don Palmer himself—and not with the girls."

"Maybe... maybe Brandi caught her doing something red-handed," said Ellie suddenly.

"What do you mean 'red-handed'?"

"Well, think of all the recent pranks and strange things happening," said Ellie, warming to her idea. "Someone was obviously trying to sabotage the contest and scare the girls. Maybe that was Sandy; maybe she decided that she needed to get more hands-on than just waving a placard. Like that trampoline on the catamaran, for example—maybe Sandy was the one who tampered with the stitches on the fastenings!"

"Oh, don't be ridiculous," said Aunt Olive. "How would she even have known that the girls were going out on that boat?"

"She could have asked around and found out. There must have been a lot of gossip about the contest at the resort and around the marina. It probably wouldn't have been that hard to find out which catamaran had been chartered for the trip, and then she could have simply gone to the marina last night, sneaked onto the boat, and cut several of the stiches along the seams. Then the weight of the girls on the trampoline would put stress on the fabric, causing it to rip open."

"Sandy would never do something like that!" declared Aunt Olive. "That wasn't a small prank. It was dangerous. Amber was lucky but she could have just as easily been caught in the propellers when she went under and been killed."

"Yes, which is exactly why Sandy can't afford to let anyone find out that she was the one who did it, otherwise she could be labeled a murderer. If Brandi found out about it somehow, Sandy could have decided that she had to silence her!"

"So you mean she committed murder to avoid being called a murderer?" said Aunt Olive sarcastically.

Ellie gave a sheepish smile. "Well, OK, my theory isn't perfect. I'm still working out the details… Fine!" she said as Aunt Olive snorted. "Fine, if you don't think it's Sandy, then who do *you* think could have done it?"

Aunt Olive shrugged. "It could have been a fellow contestant. Brandi was tipped to win, wasn't she?

Maybe one of the other girls decided to eliminate the strongest competition. That tall girl with the auburn hair—what's her name? I noticed quite a lot of tension between her and Brandi when I was watching them on the catamaran."

"You mean Amber Lopez," said Ellie thoughtfully. "Yeah, I overheard them sniping at each other several times. But do you really think Amber would commit murder just to win the contest?"

"It's well known that female rivalry can be vicious," said Aunt Olive. "Where was Amber at the time of the murder?"

"In her treatment room."

"And where was that?"

"On the other side of Brandi's room," said Ellie. "My room was on one side and Amber's room was on the other. But now that you mention it..." She looked up excitedly. "There was a connecting door between Amber's room and Brandi's! I remember now because when the therapist screamed, several people rushed in from the corridor, but Amber came in through the connecting door."

Aunt Olive raised her eyebrows. "Alone? Wasn't she with her beauty therapist?"

Ellie struggled to recall. "There was so much confusion and so many people rushing into the room... I'm not totally sure... I think I remember Amber coming in through the connecting door alone. I suppose her therapist could have gone out of her room for a moment. Mine did."

Aunt Olive's eyes gleamed. "So Amber was left alone and she had direct access through the connecting door. She could have easily slipped into Brandi's room, done the deed, and then slipped back next door. Then she could have rushed back in when you discovered the body and pretended to be shocked."

"She didn't look like she was pretending," protested Ellie, thinking of the scene that morning. "She really *did* look shocked. In fact, all the girls did. A couple of them got really hysterical. The spa had called Blake, of course, and he ended up spending more time calming the other girls down than helping with Brandi's body."

Aunt Olive didn't seem to be listening, though. She was musing to herself and now she said: "Brandi was suffocated, wasn't she?"

Ellie nodded. "Detective Carson thinks the murderer used one of the big cushions from the armchair by the French door. The murderer held it down on Brandi's face while she was lying on the bed."

She shuddered at the image that came to mind. Then she remembered the way Mojito had suddenly jumped up, all hackles raised, and stared at the adjoining wall between her room and Brandi's. With her more sensitive hearing, the cat had probably sensed the murderer next door or maybe even heard what was going on.

Brandi was probably being murdered right next

door to me and I didn't even realize! thought Ellie queasily.

"Are they sure it was the cushion?" Aunt Olive asked, interrupting her thoughts.

"Well, Carson said they'll need Forensics to confirm, but he's pretty confident that they'll find fibers from the cushion in Brandi's nose or mouth."

"That's perfect!" said Aunt Olive. "If the cushion was the murder weapon, that means anyone who could have slipped into that room unseen could have killed her. The most likely person is Amber, of course, as she could have used the connecting door, but it could just as easily have been one of the other girls..."

Or Gina, thought Ellie suddenly. She recalled catching a glimpse of the other woman going back into the steam room, just when she—Ellie—had stepped out into the corridor. *Where had Gina been? What had she been doing?*

"Did you hear what I said, poppet?"

Ellie jumped and gave her aunt an apologetic look. "Sorry—my mind drifted for a moment."

"I was asking if any of the other girls saw anything suspicious, either before or after you discovered Brandi's body?"

Ellie shrugged. "I don't know. Both the resort security and the police tried to ask that this morning, but they didn't really get anything useful out of the girls." She rolled her eyes. "Half the contestants were hysterical and the other half were spouting all sorts of wild theories about hexes or serial killers with a grudge against bikini contestants."

"And you're sure you didn't see anyone else, poppet, when you were out in the corridor?"

Ellie hesitated. "I did see Gina... but she wasn't in the corridor. She was just returning to the steam room when I stepped out. I saw the back of her, just before her door shut."

Aunt Olive raised her eyebrows. "Wasn't that a bit of a coincidence?"

"What d'you mean?"

"Well, based on the timeline of events, it means that she was outside her room at the time that Brandi was killed."

"The police questioned everyone and they aren't treating her as a suspect, though," Ellie pointed out. "So I suppose she must have a good explanation."

"Oh, the police!" Aunt Olive waved a contemptuous hand. "They've made up their minds that Sandy is guilty and I know they won't bother much to follow other leads. But they're wrong. Sandy isn't a killer and, while they're busy trying to pin the murder on her, the real culprit is getting away with it!" She looked earnestly at Ellie. "It's up to us, poppet."

"Up to us, what?"

"To solve the mystery! To find out who really murdered Brandi."

"Ohhh no!" said Ellie firmly. "I'm not getting involved in another murder investigation. Christmas is just around the corner and then I'll be going back to England in the new year—I want to enjoy the last few weeks of my vacation without being trapped in freezers, drowned in the resort pool, or eaten by alligators, thank you very much!"

Aunt Olive tutted. "My goodness, Ellie, where's your sense of adventure? I thought you came out to Florida for a bit of challenge and excitement."

"Yes, of the sun, sea, and sand variety—not the doom, danger, and death variety," retorted Ellie. "*You* can go off sleuthing if you like, Aunt Olive, but I'm not getting involved."

"But I need your help, poppet! You're already friendly with the girls—you've been helping with their photoshoots—and besides, you're about the same age. It's much easier for *you* to get close to them, to snoop around and ask questions. It would look strange if a sixty-four-year-old woman suddenly started hanging around a group of young girls, trying to get chummy with them." When Ellie didn't respond, Aunt Olive added in a provocative tone: "And what if it's Gina? What if *she's* the murderer?"

"I... She's not," said Ellie quickly.

Aunt Olive shot her a sly look. "Are you *sure?*"

"Erm... don't you think it's time we went to dinner?" asked Ellie, trying to change the subject.

Aunt Olive blinked. "Dinner? It's barely five o'clock!"

"Well... I'm starving," said Ellie. "We can pretend we're having tea."

Aunt Olive chuckled. "I doubt you'll find finger sandwiches and scones here, poppet—"

"Oh, no, I meant 'high tea,' like British farmers used to have for their evening meal in the olden days."

"Not so much of the 'olden days' and 'used to have,' young lady," said Aunt Olive tartly. "Millions of people still have 'high tea' every day all over the U.K., especially in the countryside. Not what they serve in fancy hotels nowadays, though, like those silly cucumber sandwiches and petits fours on cake stands—can you imagine a farmer eating that at the end of a hardworking day? Oh no, you had proper food, like meat pies and cold meats and bread and butter."

"Oh. So why is it called 'high tea'?" asked Ellie. "I thought it was because the food was posh and dainty."

Aunt Olive laughed. "It's only called 'high tea' because it was eaten at the dining table, rather than on low coffee tables. But you're right about the time, poppet—high tea is usually sometime between five and seven."

"OK, so we can have Florida 'high tea' with conch fritters and Key Lime Pie instead of scones and meat pies," said Ellie, grinning. "In fact, I heard that *Hammerheads* has some new specials on their menu. We haven't been there for a few nights and it'll be nice to see Sol again. We could have Happy Hour cocktails out on their terrace... what d'you say?"

CHAPTER EIGHT

Sol, the head waiter at *Hammerheads Bar and Grill,* was delighted to see them, and as Ellie looked at the kindly African-American man, with his warm smile and his twinkling black eyes, she felt a twinge of sadness. She would miss Sol when she went back to England; he had become a good friend, and chatting with him had become a happy part of her routine at the resort.

"I heard about what happened at the spa this morning," said Sol with a sympathetic look at Ellie as he led them to a table on the terrace overlooking the pool. He shook his head. "Bad business. Mr. Papadopoulos will be real upset when he gets back and hears that there's been another murder at the resort."

Aunt Olive leaned toward him and said in a stage

whisper: "Have you heard anything on the resort grapevine, Sol? Any news on the murder suspects?"

He scratched his head. "Last thing I heard was that the police had taken one of the guests in for questioning. One of the reception girls has been telling everyone about it, says the woman's some kind of crazy feminist who caused a ruckus in the lobby yesterday. Says she's real violent and dangerous—"

Aunt Olive gasped indignantly. "Those are outright lies! Sandy O'Brien is not violent or dangerous at all!"

"Oh... uh... I didn't realize you knew her, ma'am," said Sol, looking uncomfortable.

"Well, I only met Sandy yesterday," Aunt Olive admitted. "But we've become good friends. I like her—she's got spirit and she isn't afraid to speak her mind and stand up for what she believes in." She wagged a finger at Sol. "Sandy is a kind, caring woman who is just being used by the police as a scapegoat! I know she's not the murderer! You tell the other resort staff that all those rumors about her are untrue—d'you hear me? I'm counting on you, Sol, to stop these vicious lies and change everyone's view of Sandy."

"Uh... I'll try my best, ma'am," said Sol, looking even more uneasy now.

"How's Jasmine?" asked Ellie, feeling sorry for him and trying to change the subject.

Sol beamed at the mention of his daughter. "She's

great, thanks. You know, I actually think something good came out of what happened and the traumatic experience you guys had. Having a brush with murder and death sure puts things in perspective! Jasmine hasn't been going out to parties so much or hanging out with the 'wild crowd' anymore. She's been saving up and she's talking about taking a road trip with her friend Ava before starting college next fall. I think it'll be a good experience for the two of them."

"It sounds wonderful," said Ellie with a wistful sigh. "I wanted to have a 'gap year' between leaving school and starting uni, but I didn't, and now I really regret it. You're only eighteen once in your life!"

Sol smiled. "Well, if you decide to stay after the new year, I'm sure there would be a seat in their car waiting for you. In fact, Jasmine keeps pestering me to remind you that she's still up for that trip to Disney World whenever you like."

"I just might take her up on that," said Ellie, chuckling. "It would be terrible to go back to England without visiting at least one of the famous Orlando theme parks."

Sol took their orders, then left them to enjoy their cocktails on the outdoor terrace. The sun was just slipping over the horizon—a glowing ball of red amid a sky washed with brilliant hues of coral and orange. The beach was mostly in shadow, but the last of the sun's rays touched the backs of the waves with a golden glow as they rolled onto the shore. The silhouettes of palm trees framed the view, dark and distinct against the vivid sky.

It was a scene straight from a postcard and Ellie sighed with pleasure as she leaned back and sipped her drink. Her gaze wandered away from the beach, toward the people walking past the restaurant: they were either heading for the pool deck or down one of the walkways leading to the other facilities in the resort grounds. She loved people-watching and the Sunset Palms Beach Resort, with its wide variety of guests, was the perfect place to do it. Aunt Olive usually delighted in joining Ellie in speculating about passing guests, but tonight she seemed unusually quiet.

Then suddenly she burst out: "We have to do something! We can't let poor Sandy be wrongfully blamed for this murder!"

Ellie sighed. "Aunt Olive—" She broke off as she heard her name being called. Turning in her seat and peering over the edge of the terrace, she saw a group of girls standing on the pool deck, waving to her: the bikini pageant contestants.

"Hi Ellie! We're going down to the Snack Shack to watch the sunset. Wanna join us?" Kimberley called.

"Yeah, we're gonna sit around the fire pit and roast some s'mores," said Destiny eagerly. "You gotta come!"

Ellie was surprised and touched by the invitation. "Oh! Thanks, that's really sweet of you," she said. "I'd love to but—"

"She's joining you right away," Aunt Olive called, her louder voice cutting across Ellie's.

Ellie turned to look at her aunt. "But I can't. I've just ordered food and besides—"

"This is the perfect opportunity!" Aunt Olive hissed. "You can't pass it up!"

"But—"

Before Ellie realized what was happening, her aunt had hustled her out of her chair and was bundling her to the restaurant entrance, where she was practically shoved off the terrace and into the group of waiting girls.

"Toodle-oo! Have a good time with your friends, dear," cooed Aunt Olive, waving. "Don't worry about rushing back tonight. I'll just be having a quiet evening in with my... er... knitting."

"Aww, she's so sweet, your aunt," said Sharlene.

Sweet? Ellie gave Aunt Olive a wry look. 'Sweet' was the last word she would've used. Devious and stubborn, maybe! What's more, she was sure that Aunt Olive had never knitted a day in her whole life!

Still, there was nothing she could do but join the girls. It would have looked too strange and rude if she backed out now. And a part of her had to admit that she *was* flattered by the invitation. The bikini contestants were so pretty and glamorous, with their perfect figures and alluring looks. Ellie felt like the school nerd who had been invited to join the "popular girls'" group.

Anyway, just because I'm going with them doesn't

mean I'll be working on the mystery, she reminded herself. *I'm just going to enjoy some snacks, make some new friends, and have a good time.*

She fell into step beside Roxy, who was bringing up the rear of the group, and joined in the general chatter. Everyone seemed to have recovered from the shock and hysteria of that morning, although they were still slightly subdued overall. Ellie was a bit surprised at first to note that their distress seemed to be more centered around concerns for their own safety—with the murderer still at large—rather than any genuine grief for the dead girl. From their comments, Ellie gathered that, despite the time they'd spent together in the last few weeks during the run-up to the contest finale, Brandi hadn't been liked by any of the other girls and wasn't really going to be missed. So maybe it wasn't so surprising after all that they were joking and laughing so soon after her death.

They made their way past the pool deck and down the path to the beach. There was an area at the edge of the resort grounds, just before the open sand, which had been left in its natural state. Here, sea oats and other beach grasses grew in thick tussocks between rolling sand dunes, and palm trees leaned haphazardly amongst clumps of railroad vines and other seashore vegetation. And in the midst of this "wild" environment was one of the resort's more unusual eateries—a little beachcomber shack serving iconic snacks from the different states around America.

Ellie had only been to the Snack Shack in the daytime before and, even then, she had been charmed by the rustic setting. Now, in the fading light of the setting sun, she looked at the wooden shack in the distance with delight. A collection of driftwood, empty oil barrels, and wooden crates did duty as makeshift chairs and tables around the shack, although most people seemed to be huddled around one of the glowing fire pits set in the sand. The mouthwatering smell of crispy, deep-fried snacks drifted over on the breeze, and Ellie's stomach growled, reminding her that she'd left her dinner with Aunt Olive back at *Hammerheads Bar and Grill.*

"Erm… are we going to have other foods besides these s'mores things?" she asked as they made their way across the last dune.

Kimberley turned back to look at her. "Why would you want to eat anything else when there's s'mores?" she said, giggling.

"Are they really that good?" asked Ellie skeptically.

"Omigod, you've never had s'mores?" gasped Nikki.

Ellie shook her head. "It's a North American thing. I'd never really heard of them until I came to the U.S. They're a kind of toasted marshmallow, aren't they?"

"Oh no, s'mores are so much more than that," exclaimed Sharlene.

"I can't believe you've never had them—you've been, like, missing out your whole life!" cried Destiny.

The other girls nodded vehemently.

"Well, I'll try and make up for it tonight," said Ellie, chuckling.

"Don't worry, just in case you don't like them, there'll be loads of other food as well," Roxy added. "Gina's meeting us there and she said if she arrived first, she would order a bunch of things from the menu."

"Gina's coming too?" said Ellie, dismayed.

"Yeah, and apparently she's bringing her boyfriend," Sharlene giggled.

"Her *ex*-boyfriend," said Amber. "Although I can see why she'd want him back—he's really hot! He's the resident doc here at the resort—"

"Omigod, you mean the guy who came to see us at the spa this morning?"

"That's him?"

"Dr. Blake Thornton... oh my God, he's sooo cute!"

"Yeah, he was so awesome. I was, like, really freaking out and he was so patient with me."

"Me too. He really calmed me down."

"You were flirting with him so bad."

"I was not!"

"Yes, you were—you were, like, all over him."

"It's no use, anyway; he's taken," said Amber.

The other girls turned wide eyes on her. "How do you know?"

"'Cos he told me," said Amber. "I went to his clinic yesterday after we got back from the catamaran, so he could check me over for any serious injuries, and I tried to flirt with him—you know, ask him if he'd be free for a drink later or something—and he was polite and nice and all, but he made it really clear that he wasn't interested."

"Maybe he just wasn't interested in *you*, Amber," said one of the other girls slyly.

Amber shot her a challenging look. "No man ever turns me down unless he's already fallen for someone else."

"So you mean he's got a girlfriend?" said Kimberley, looking very disappointed.

"He didn't come out and say he had a girlfriend," said Amber, frowning. "But I got the impression that there was someone here at the resort."

Ellie had been listening in an uncomfortable silence, but now she felt her face reddening, and she was glad of the fading light which made it difficult for the others to see her clearly.

"Maybe it's Gina, then," said Destiny. "Maybe he's thinking about getting back with her."

"No way! They're definitely not together," said Sharlene.

Nikki giggled. "Yeah, but have you seen the way she looks at him? She definitely *wishes* they were!"

"If that's the case, you'd better not flirt with him, Amber," said Kimberley jokingly. "I wouldn't wanna go after any man that Gina has her eyes on!"

Amber put a hand on her hips. "Oh yeah? You think I'm scared of her? If I really wanted to, I bet I could steal Blake away from her."

"What do you think, Ellie?" Roxy asked, turning bright eyes on her.

"Erm... I... I don't know..." Ellie mumbled, keeping her head down.

She felt horribly torn and embarrassed. It seemed too arrogant and presumptuous to speak up and claim that *she* could be the mysterious woman who had captured Blake Thornton's heart. The last thing she wanted was to be the target of the other girls' salacious curiosity. But on the other hand, if they discovered later that she and Blake had been spending time together, it would look like she had deliberately deceived them by being coy about her involvement with the handsome doctor.

Arrgh! thought Ellie in frustration. *As if things aren't complicated enough already!*

CHAPTER NINE

Ellie's heart sank when they arrived at the Snack Shack and she saw Gina sitting at one of the fire pits with Blake beside her. The blonde woman waved and beckoned them over, although a flash of annoyance crossed her face when she saw Ellie. She hid it quickly, however, and said in a smooth voice:

"Ellie! How nice to see you. I didn't realize you were joining us."

"We saw her over by the pool and invited her along," Kimberley explained.

"She's never tasted s'mores before; can you believe it?" said Destiny.

"Oh, we've got to fix that right away," said Blake with a smile, standing up and coming toward Ellie. "It's great to see you, Ellie—I feel like I haven't seen you in days!"

Ellie was aware of Gina's hard gaze on her, as well as the other girls' sudden interest, and she found herself blushing. She hoped the darkness would hide the flush on her face.

"Oh... I'm... I'm sure we've seen each other... erm... around the resort," she stammered. "And... I was at the spa this morning, remember?"

At the mention of the spa, Blake's face sobered. "That was different."

Ellie ducked her head. "Yes. Sorry. You're right. Have you been tied up with the police all day?"

Blake grimaced. "Most of it, anyway. With Mr. Papadopoulos away, most of the decisions seem to be falling to me. Of course, I'm officially the resort doctor, not the manager—that's Gil Anderson and he's great at his job—but since Detective Carson has dealt with me several times before, the police seem to be more comfortable liaising with me."

"Oh, let's not talk about the murder investigation," said Gina quickly. "The whole point of coming here tonight is to forget what happened this morning and have fun! Sit down... sit down..." She gestured to the spaces around the fire pit and the girls followed her bidding.

Ellie dropped down beside one of the girls and Blake moved to sit next to her, but Gina darted in and quickly took the spot beside Ellie. This meant that Blake had no choice but to take the last empty space—which was beside Gina, at the edge of the circle. It also meant that he was effectively cut off from the rest of the girls, as Gina turned toward him and launched into an animated conversation, demanding all his attention. Ellie found herself looking at Gina's back as the blonde woman deliberately turned away from her and hunched her shoulders, so that Ellie was excluded from the conversation.

Ellie felt a surge of annoyance, then she took a deep breath and let it out slowly. *I'm not here to get into a catfight over a man*, she told herself. Calmly, she turned in the opposite direction, toward the girl on her other side—who happened to be Nikki—and watched with interest as Nikki began busily assembling several items in front of her.

"What are you doing?" Ellie asked.

"I'm making s'mores," said Nikki.

"Here... you can try too," said Kimberley from beyond Nikki, passing across some items.

Ellie looked down in bemusement at the pile of things she had been handed. There was a small stack of thin, rectangular crackers, a large, flat bar of chocolate, and a pile of marshmallows, as well as a long skewer.

"Do I just put them all on the skewer?" she asked.

"No, no, you get a piece of graham cracker and lay it down first, like this," said Roxy from the other side of the fire as she demonstrated with her own cracker. "Then you break off a piece of chocolate and lay it on top."

"And then you toast a marshmallow over the fire,"

Kimberley continued, showing how she'd pushed a marshmallow onto her skewer and was now holding it out over the flames.

"Be careful not to burn them, though!" said Destiny.

"Yeah, you need to rotate the skewer, so that the marshmallow's evenly toasted on all sides," said Roxy helpfully.

"And then you put the marshmallow on the chocolate, lay another graham cracker on top, and hold it down while you pull the skewer out!" said Nikki, demonstrating with flourish. She held up what looked like a miniature sandwich, with melted marshmallow and chocolate oozing out from between the two layers of graham crackers. "Ta-da! Here—go on! Taste it!"

Ellie gingerly took the sticky mass and bit into the s'more. The warm, melted marshmallow combined with the chocolate in a deliciously sweet, gooey mouthful, accompanied by the crisp crunch of the graham crackers. She looked up to see all the girls watching her with bated breath.

"Well?" said Roxy, her eyes bright.

Ellie nodded, trying to speak with her mouth full. "Mmm... it's delicious!" she mumbled.

"Told ya!" said Kimberley, grinning. "You'll be addicted now."

Ellie swallowed and laughed. "I think you might be right. I don't know what I'm going to do when I get back home."

"Can't you make s'mores in England?" asked Nikki.

"We've got marshmallows... and chocolate, of course. But I don't think we have these," said Ellie, holding up one of the graham crackers. "The closest thing I can think of is a digestive biscuit but—aside from being round instead of rectangular—they're a different texture." She nibbled experimentally on the edge of a cracker. "Also, graham crackers have more of a... malty-cinnamony flavor, I think? Anyway, I'm not sure how digestives would taste with melted marshmallows," she added with a doubtful look.

"How d'you eat them, then?" asked Sharlene curiously.

"Oh, well, the traditional way is dunked in tea."

"*What?*" The girls looked horrified.

"You mean... you dip them in a cup of tea?"

"But don't they go all wet and soggy?"

"That's the whole point," said Ellie, chuckling. "You dunk them in hot, milky tea and then eat them as fast as you can, before they disintegrate."

Amber looked disgusted. "That's just dumb," she said.

Ellie was slightly taken aback by the girl's rudeness, but she pretended not to hear and continued: "My favorite is chocolate digestives— those are the ones with chocolate coated on one side. The chocolate melts in the hot tea and it's even more delicious!"

Seeing the girls' stupefied expressions around

her, she laughed and said: "Don't knock it till you've tried it!" She picked up her skewer. "Right—now I'm going to make a s'more myself."

Ellie tried to follow the same steps the girls had shown her, but she had barely started to toast her marshmallow when it caught fire.

"Yikes!" cried Ellie, jerking her skewer out of the flames and staring at her burning marshmallow in dismay. The outside edges were already turning black and sooty.

"I think you're gonna have to throw that one out and start again," said Kimberley with a sympathetic look.

"No way! The ones that are a bit burnt are the best," declared Sharlene.

"I think this is a lot more than 'a bit burnt,'" said Ellie ruefully, looking at the charred lump that was now on the end of her skewer. She knocked it off and pushed a fresh marshmallow onto the prongs. This time, she took care not to hold the skewer too deep into the fire, and rotated it steadily. She was rewarded a few minutes later with a beautifully toasted marshmallow: soft and gooey on the inside but with a crispy, golden-cinnamon coating on the outside. She placed this on her stack of graham cracker and chocolate, like she'd been shown, sandwiched the whole thing with another graham cracker, then—with some fumbling—managed to pull the skewer out without dragging the marshmallow out as well, although she did smear a lot of it over the edges of the cracker.

"Not bad for a first try," said Nikki, leaning over to look with a smile.

After that, Ellie became a pro, vying with the other girls to see who could toast a marshmallow and create a s'more the fastest. By the time they set down their skewers a while later, Ellie was feeling slightly sick from all the chocolate and marshmallow she had consumed!

"You still want any other food?" asked Roxy with a grin from the other side of the fire.

Ellie shook her head. "Bloody hell, no! I feel like I won't need to eat for another week!"

"We shouldn't really be eating s'mores now either," admitted Nikki. "We're all supposed to be, like, watching our figures, you know, to make sure we're in perfect shape for the contest."

"Yeah, I told you this was a dumb idea," said Amber, standing up abruptly. "I'm going back."

Without another word, she turned and stalked off, heading across the dunes toward the main resort building. Ellie stared after her in surprise. She had noticed that Amber hadn't said much or joined the general banter. The auburn-haired girl had held herself aloof from the other girls and declined to make any s'mores. But Ellie hadn't thought too much of it; she had been having too much fun herself to pay the sullen girl any attention. Now, though, she watched thoughtfully as Amber disappeared into the distance.

"Whoa... looks like Miss Queen Bee is in a mood tonight," said Kimberley, making a face at Amber's retreating back.

Nikki shrugged. "Well, it's nicer without her anyway."

"Yeah, she's such a *bi-atch*," said Sharlene in an exaggerated tone.

"I'm always a little nervous when she's around anyway," confessed Destiny.

"Me too," said Roxy in a small voice. "And I have to share a room with her."

"What d'you mean?" said Ellie, surprised.

Destiny exchanged a look with the other girls before saying to Ellie: "You just don't wanna get on Amber's bad side."

Ellie frowned. "Are you saying that you're... scared of her?"

"Not scared, exactly," said Nikki quickly. "Just more... like... careful."

Kimberley nodded. "Yeah, Amber can be really mean."

"More than mean," said Sharlene with a dark look. Then, as everyone kept silent, she burst out in a frustrated voice: "Aww, come on! We're all thinking it even if no one wants to say it!"

"Thinking what?" asked Ellie, although she had an inkling.

Sharlene hesitated, then, after a wary glance at Gina—who was still engrossed in conversation with Blake—she lowered her voice and said: "We think

Amber could have done it."

Ellie stared at her. Then she looked at the scared faces of the other girls around the fire. She knew she'd said she wouldn't get involved, but she found her curiosity piqued in spite of herself. Before she realized what she was doing, she was saying:

"You think Amber murdered Brandi?"

CHAPTER TEN

The other girls all looked at each other uncomfortably.

"Well... maybe not on purpose," said Kimberley, shifting uneasily. "But... you know... like, maybe they had a fight and it was an accident—"

"How do you smother someone with a cushion by accident?" asked Ellie, unable to keep the sarcastic note out of her voice.

"Maybe Amber didn't mean to kill Brandi. Maybe she just meant to scare her but then it got out of hand."

"But why would she want to 'scare' Brandi?" asked Ellie.

The girls exchanged glances again, then Sharlene said:

"They had a pretty big fight the night before. I

mean, they'd been, like, sniping at each other all day, you know, but it got worse after we got back from the catamaran. After dinner, we were all sitting around in Brandi's room—she had the most space, you see, 'cos she was the only one of us without a roommate—"

"Yeah, and that really annoyed Amber. She thought Brandi was getting special treatment and she was so jealous," said Destiny.

"It was just the way the rooms got handed out," said Kimberley. "'Cos there's, like, seven of us, right? So one of us had to be in a room on her own. Brandi drew the lucky straw. But Amber didn't believe it. She thought Brandi must have gone behind our backs and sucked up to Mr. Palmer or something—"

"Yeah, like 'sucked up' literally!" said Sharlene with a meaningful look and a snicker. "That's what Amber said to Brandi. She called Brandi a slut and said she knew what Brandi was giving Mr. Palmer in exchange for the special treatment."

"And then Brandi said: 'It takes one to know one'—which really triggered Amber! She went nuts! We had to grab her and hold her back, 'cos we thought she was gonna scratch Brandi's eyes out," said Nikki, shaking her head at the memory.

"What did Brandi do?" asked Ellie. "Was she scared?"

"Nah, she just laughed in Amber's face and said she was gonna report the whole thing. Then she flounced out of the room and went off to find Gina."

"And that's when I heard Amber say it," said Sharlene.

"Say what?" asked Ellie.

"She sort of muttered under her breath: 'Just you wait...'"

"That's it? She didn't say anything else?" asked Ellie, disappointed.

"What else did she need to say?" Nikki replied. "It's obvious, right? She was planning to get even."

"By *murdering* Brandi? Isn't that a bit extreme?" said Ellie skeptically.

The girls shrugged. "You don't know Amber."

Ellie thought for a moment. "But didn't you all say that you thought someone was sabotaging the whole contest and stalking you? Well, if the saboteur and the murderer are the same person, then how do you explain what happened to Amber on the catamaran? *She* was the girl who was threatened."

"Maybe she staged it herself," Roxy spoke up in a timid voice. "I mean... you could do something like that to make yourself look like a victim."

Ellie stared at the other girl, her own thoughts whirling. She hadn't considered that possibility, but Roxy was right. If Amber had sabotaged the trampoline, she would have known exactly where the weakness in the fabric was. Ellie thought back to the way Amber had eagerly bounced on the trampoline. At the time, she'd just thought that the girl was keen to perform for the camera, but maybe it had all been part of Amber's ploy? If she had been prepared and knew exactly what was going to happen, the risks could have been minimal. Amber knew that she was a strong swimmer and, when she fell into the water, she probably dived deep to avoid the propellers and come up some distance away from the boat...

"What are you guys talking about?"

The girls all jumped guiltily and looked up to see that Gina was leaning over to look at them with a falsely bright smile. Ellie glanced around in surprise, wondering where Blake had gone, then saw him at a neighboring fire pit talking to a couple whose toddler seemed to have hurt his finger. Gina shuffled closer to the rest of the girls and looked expectantly at them.

"Uh... nothing much!" said Kimberley quickly. "Just... just talking about what happened on the catamaran yesterday."

Nikki spoke up: "Miss Ross—"

"Oh, I told you all to call me Gina," said Gina with a false camaraderie.

"Gina," Nikki said instead. "Do you know what's going on with the contest? We were supposed to have our big finale and catwalk stage show the day after tomorrow."

"Well, I had a discussion with Mr. Palmer and Detective Carson this evening and, unfortunately, they're saying the contest has to be put on hold while the murder investigation is ongoing."

The girls gasped and gave cries of dismay.

"What?"

"Nooo!"

"They can't do that!"

"How long are they going to put it on hold?"

"What are we gonna do? We can't hang around at the resort forever!"

"Don't worry, I've figured something out," said Gina smoothly. "I don't think the delay will be more than a few days—a week at the most—and in the meantime, I think we can take advantage of the situation, turn the contest into something much more like a reality TV show. We could hire a film crew and get footage of you girls here at the resort. You know, maybe do more photoshoots in different settings or just show you girls hanging out, trying different resort activities. It'll be like these model talent shows you see on TV."

There were squeals and cries of delight from the girls and they all looked at each other excitedly.

"I'll need to clear it with Mr. Palmer because a film crew will require a bigger budget. But if I can get one of the networks on board, then I think I should be able to swing it," said Gina. "I'm sure Mr. Palmer will see the benefits of the extra exposure."

"But how are you gonna get a network interested?" asked Kimberley.

"Oh, that's easy," said Gina with a complacent smile. "Brandi's murder has been big news. I'm sure networks will be falling over themselves to get exclusive rights to live coverage from the resort. And audiences will love it! They'll want to see how you girls are coping with the stress and whether someone else gets targeted... It'll be like *Survivor* meets *America's Next Top Model*—it'll be awesome!"

"Don't you think it's a bit immoral exploiting Brandi's murder like that?" asked Ellie with distaste.

"The girl's dead already. Nothing's going to bring her back," answered Gina coolly. She glanced at her watch, then said to the girls: "We'd better be heading back. There's room service, so you can snack if you get hungry later, but I suggest you all get an early night. I've booked the photographer to come back first thing in the morning—we might try to do a photoshoot on a hammock by the beach. It'll produce great publicity shots, even if it isn't filmed."

The girls gathered their things and started back toward the main resort building, talking excitedly as they went. Ellie followed them, but she had barely gone a few steps when she heard her name being called. She glanced back to see that Blake had returned from the other fire pit and was hurriedly trying to catch up with her.

"Hi..." He smiled at her as he fell into step next to her. "Sorry, we never really got a chance to talk."

That's because Gina completely monopolized you, like a she-dog guarding a juicy bone, thought Ellie. Then she felt slightly ashamed of her catty thoughts. Giving Blake an understanding look, she said: "That's OK. I was having fun making s'mores with the other girls."

"It looked like you were getting very good at it,

from what I saw," said Blake, chuckling. "Maybe we could come back another night and you could show *me* how to do it," he added teasingly. "Hey, listen— while we're on the subject: are you free tomorrow night?"

"Yes, why?"

"Well, we never made it to that fish shack I wanted to take you to last time. How about we give it another go?"

Ellie glanced back at Gina, who had been held up by one of the staff members from the Snack Shack. "What about Gina?"

"What about her?"

"I thought..." Ellie swallowed, trying to keep the jealous note out of her voice. "Well, since she's here at the resort... and you used to be together... maybe you'd want to go out to dinner with her—"

"I want to go out to dinner with *you*," said Blake, his brown eyes intent.

Before Ellie could answer, Gina caught up with them, sidling artfully between them so that she was walking between Ellie and Blake.

"What have I missed?" she said, a bright smile pinned on her face. "You know, Blake, your boss is so sweet! Apparently, he told the staff at the Snack Shack to let us have snacks any time on the house."

"Yeah, Mr. Papadopoulos is a great guy," Blake agreed. "I heard that he was the one who offered the spa treatments this morning?"

"Yes, and I was so looking forward to a bit of

pampering! Who knew that a *murder* would happen?" Gina gave a dramatic sigh and passed a hand over her eyes. "Oh honey, it's been the most awful couple of days! First all the challenges of organizing this event, then the accident on the catamaran yesterday... and now there's a murder investigation and I have to face the media..." Her voice wobbled and she threw Blake a limpid look. "I just don't know how I'm going to cope!"

He gave her a reassuring pat on the shoulder. "You'll be fine, Gina—"

"Oh Blake!" Gina leaned quickly toward him, falling against his chest. Blake was taken by surprise and looked embarrassed as Gina snaked her arms around his neck and snuggled closer.

She's practically trying to worm into his chest, thought Ellie in disgust as she watched the other woman cling to Blake. The helpless-little-girl act was so completely at odds with the ruthless and capable woman Ellie had seen earlier, that it was obvious that it was all put on for Blake's benefit.

Blake patted Gina's back awkwardly. "I'm sure you'll do great, Gina. You always do."

Gina sniffed and kept her head down, her voice muffled as she said: "Thanks. It's just so hard, you know... I suppose it's silly of me, but I got used to having someone to share my troubles with... and now I'm all alone..." She trailed off meaningfully.

Blake cleared his throat. "If you need me to help with anything, Gina, you know where to find me." He reached up and gently untangled her arms from around his neck, easing her away.

"Oh, there's something that would *really* help," said Gina quickly. "I feel like I just need to get away from the resort for a while, to clear my head and relax." She gave Blake a coy look. "I was thinking... maybe we could go get a bite to eat together? I haven't seen anything of Tampa Bay since arriving last week. I thought you would have taken me out to show me a couple local places by now, but you're always 'working,'" she added, pouting. "How about tonight? The evening's still young."

Blake shook his head. "Sorry, I've been busy with the police all day and I've got a lot of catching up to do at the clinic—patient notes to dictate and things like that."

"OK, how about tomorrow night, then?" said Gina brightly.

Blake shook his head again. "I've got plans tomorrow night—I'm taking Ellie out to dinner."

Gina drew in her breath sharply, then she said: "Oh, I'm sure Ellie wouldn't mind if you guys took a raincheck. I mean, she's on vacation, right? She's just sitting around, not doing anything... whereas I'm dealing with a really difficult situation here!" She looked up at Blake, her eyes huge. "Honey, I really need to de-stress."

Blake hesitated, then he said firmly, "I'm sorry, but I can't change my plans. I've already had to postpone too many times. I'm taking Ellie out to dinner tomorrow night; otherwise, after that, I'll be on-call for a few nights and won't be able to leave the resort."

"Oh. Well..." Gina smiled through gritted teeth, although her eyes glinted as she looked at Ellie. "I guess we'll have to do it another time."

Ellie shifted uncomfortably. A part of her was flattered by Blake's commitment to their date, but another part felt awkward and embarrassed to be caught in the middle of a clichéd triangle. And from the venomous look that Gina had shot her, she wondered if she had made a bad enemy.

CHAPTER ELEVEN

The next morning, Ellie was woken by the shrill ringing of the phone. She groaned as she heaved herself out of bed to answer it and groaned even more when she heard her older sister's voice on the other end of the line.

"Karen! Do you realize what time it is?"

"Oh… it's just gone past noon in London so it must be around seven a.m. in Florida?" said her sister airily. "Don't tell me you're still in bed?"

"Well, of course I'm still in bed!" said Ellie, sitting up grumpily. "Who on earth would be up at this time of the morning when they're on holiday?"

"When we go away, I always make sure that I get up to see the sunrise. And then I do my yoga practice or maybe get a morning jog in before Geoff and the children are up."

Ellie rolled her eyes. "Well, good for you, but the rest of us mere mortals like to relax and laze around when we're on vacation."

Karen sniffed. "It doesn't sound like you're doing much relaxing anyway."

"What d'you mean?"

"Aunt Olive rang me last night. It was nice to catch up with the old dear—I haven't spoken to her in nearly a year, I think! I must say, Ellie, she seems to get more eccentric every day. Anyway," Karen continued briskly, "she was telling me what you'd been up to and it sounds like you've been meddling in all sorts of things at the resort. Cocktail workshops and pie contests and even murder investigations!"

"I haven't been 'meddling'!" said Ellie indignantly. "I just happened to get sucked into a few things—it's not my fault. I didn't ask to get involved."

"That's not what I heard," said Karen in that disapproving voice that Ellie knew so well. "Aunt Olive said you actually *agreed* to help the resort owner snoop around and question suspects after the death at the pie contest. And then you got involved in another murder, defending one of the resort staff and doing all sorts of investigating by yourself because you didn't believe that he could be guilty."

"Well, I was right—he wasn't!" said Ellie. "And if I hadn't helped to solve that case, Sol could have ended up going to jail."

"Oh, don't be ridiculous, Ellie. I'm sure the police

would have found the culprit in the end. In any case, it's hardly your problem, is it? I would have thought that the resort would look after their own staff."

"They do... but this was different. Sol is a personal friend, not just the 'resort staff.' Anyway, I would have thought that, as a lawyer, you'd be glad I helped to prevent an innocent man being punished for a crime he didn't commit."

"Well, of course, I'm glad you contributed," said Karen dismissively. "But there's a difference. These weren't professional clients that you were paid to help. You're not a detective, Ellie. You're not even a criminal lawyer. You shouldn't be getting involved in things that you have no knowledge of or skills in."

"I've done pretty well so far," said Ellie, stung. "If it weren't for me, the police would have missed vital clues in all three cases and wouldn't have found the killers so quickly."

"Yes, but at what personal cost? I heard from Aunt Olive that you nearly got attacked by an alligator! Ellie, that isn't funny—you might have been killed! Really, it's *just* like you to be so completely ignorant and careless about things. I told you—you can't go through life lurching from one crisis to another. You need to have a plan. You need to think long-term and..."

Ellie groaned silently and put her face in her palm, tuning out her sister's voice. She knew that Karen meant well. Her sister might sound patronizing and overbearing, but ultimately it was because she cared and wanted the best for Ellie. Still, it didn't make her lecturing any easier to take.

"...and now Aunt Olive tells me there's been another death at the resort! And there's a murder investigation ongoing. Is that right?"

Ellie hurriedly pulled her attention back to the phone. "Uh... yeah, that's right."

"Well, you'd better not be thinking about getting involved again," said Karen, her voice dripping with disapproval.

Ellie hesitated. She *had* been resolved not to do any more sleuthing but now, faced with her sister's bossy ultimatum, something pricked her to say, rather defiantly:

"I don't know... I might."

Karen drew an outraged breath. "Ellie! Haven't you been listening to anything I've been saying?"

"Yes, and I'll keep it all in mind," said Ellie, quickly changing the subject. "So... how are the Christmas preparations going? It's only a couple of weeks now until Christmas Eve. Are the children getting excited? Have they started the chocolate advent calendar yet?"

"Pardon? Oh... oh yes," said Karen, momentarily distracted. "Yes, although I've decided that I'm not going to let them consume those dreadful mass-market chocolates that you find in supermarkets, full of cheap sugars and additives. So this year, I've ordered a protein ball advent calendar. It's marvelous! Twenty-four days of high-protein vegan balls, free from sugar, gluten, and soy, with an extra treat on Christmas Day made of protein pea isolate."

"Oh... erm... sounds wonderful," said Ellie, making a face and feeling deeply sorry for her little niece and nephew.

"That reminds me—you haven't told me what you want for Christmas yet. Anything you need? You know I like to get you a practical item, something that you can keep for posterity."

"I don't want or need anything really," said Ellie. She laughed. "Once I would have said a beach holiday in the sun—but that's covered now!"

"But we must get you something. We always get you something," insisted Karen. "I was thinking: if I put it in the post this weekend, it might still arrive in Florida in time for Christmas Day."

"Oh... no, don't worry about it, Karen. Honestly! It's silly going to all that trouble and the expense of sending a parcel halfway around the world. If you really want to get me something, why don't you just hold on to it until January? I'll be back soon after the new year. That's what I was planning to do with the gifts for the children," added Ellie hastily. In actual fact, she had completely forgotten about Christmas presents for her niece and nephew until now. "I... erm... was going to bring them back something special from Florida."

"But..." Karen sounded twitchy and uncomfortable. "That's not how it should be done. It's tradition to open presents on Christmas Day, after the turkey."

"Traditions can change. I mean, Christmas this year is going to be unusual anyway, what with me being in Florida, and Mum and Dad going off on a cruise, so... go on, be daring, Karen! Open some presents in January! I promise you the world won't end," said Ellie, grinning.

"Hmm... well, I hope you're not going to make a habit of gallivanting off to Florida every Christmas," said Karen peevishly. "Now, I'd better dash. Don't forget what I said, Ellie. Don't go sticking your nose in business that's none of your concern. I know you've always blundered through life without giving any thought to the consequences of your actions, but you're not a teenager anymore and you've got to start behaving more responsibly."

After Ellie hung up, she found that she was clenching her teeth and her jaw was rigid. She took a deep breath and let it out slowly, trying to ease the tension in her neck and shoulders. She knew it was silly to get so worked up. She should have been used to Karen's lecturing by now—she'd spent her whole life in her bossy older sister's shadow—and she normally turned a deaf ear to the well-meaning but patronizing advice. Still, the memory of Karen's sanctimonious tone really irked her and, when she went out into the villa's living room to find Aunt Olive reading the paper with a morning coffee, Ellie launched into her own indignant tirade.

"...I can't believe she's telling me not to meddle in

other people's business when she's happily meddling in mine!" fumed Ellie. "Honestly, I want to thump Karen sometimes! Can you believe she had the nerve to tell me not to get involved in a murder investigation again? And in that same bossy tone she always used when we were little and she expected me to do everything she said."

"And did you agree to obey?" asked Aunt Olive with a gleam in her eye.

"No, of course I didn't!" snapped Ellie. "What d'you take me for? I'm not eight years old anymore and I'm not going to be pushed around by—" She broke off suddenly and stared at her aunt. Then she gasped and said accusingly: "*Aunt Olive!* It was you, wasn't it? You set up the whole thing! You engineered it so that Karen would lecture me and I would get annoyed and be provoked into getting involved! That was why you called Karen last night, when I was out at the Snack Shack. I thought that was a bit weird."

"Nonsense! I merely wanted to speak to my other niece. What's so unusual about that?"

"Except that you *never* call Karen 'just for a chat,'" said Ellie. "You told me yourself that you never know what to say to her and it always ends up being awkward. You only ever do it once a year at Christmas or something, when you feel guilty about it."

"Rubbish!" said Aunt Olive. "I don't know where you get your ideas from, Ellie. Maybe you inherited my wild imagination." She chuckled, then stood up and drained her coffee cup. "Now, I'm going to have a shower and get dressed. I've booked a personal session with one of the tennis coaches this morning to go over the best serving techniques."

"I didn't realize you played tennis," said Ellie, furrowing her brow.

Aunt Olive gave her wink. "I don't. But then I saw the handsome young tennis coach and decided it's high time I learned..."

Ellie watched her aunt retreat to her bedroom. *Ooh, she's a devious old bat*, she thought with a mixture of exasperation and admiration. *Trust Aunt Olive to try and manipulate me. Well, she's not going to succeed. I said I'm not getting involved in this mystery and that's that!*

CHAPTER TWELVE

Ellie looked up at the sky, stretching out her arms and kicking her legs in the deliciously cool water. She could feel herself bobbing on the surface of the pool and she relished the feeling. She couldn't believe that only a few weeks ago, floating like this would have been completely beyond her. Even wading in the pool up to her chin would have probably given her a panic attack. But when she'd arrived in Florida, she had been determined to learn to swim at last and—with some patient tutoring from Blake and a lot of practice—she had finally learned how to make herself buoyant and even do a version of a dog paddle-breaststroke combo.

But the best thing was being able to float like this on her back in the pool, drifting lazily along, feeling the water lap at the sides of her cheeks and gently tug at the strands of her hair...

Ahhh... now this *is what being on vacation is all about,* thought Ellie with a happy sigh, closing her eyes. *No sleuthing, no mystery, just lazing by the pool, enjoying the balmy weather and glorious sunshine...* But even as she began to relax, something intruded on her thoughts: the memory of Karen's voice bossily telling her not to get involved. The more she thought about it, the more it niggled her. She knew that she was probably just playing into Aunt Olive's hands. It was classic reverse psychology and she hated to admit it, but it was working.

Her musings were interrupted by a raucous screeching and she opened her eyes to see a flurry of red feathers. The next moment, a scarlet macaw swooped low across the pool before coming to land on one of the handrails by the steps leading into the water. He made a loud hooting sound, bobbing his head and ruffling his feathers, obviously trying to get Ellie's attention. She tipped herself upright, feeling water stream down her hair and onto her shoulders, then waded over to the steps and looked up at the parrot with affection.

"Hello Hemingway."

"*WHATCHA' DOIN'?*" croaked the macaw, cocking his head to eye her curiously.

"I'm swimming," said Ellie. "What are *you* doing?"

"*I'M SWIMMING.*"

Ellie laughed. "No, you're not. You're being nosy." She climbed out of the pool and walked over to a nearby lounge chair, where she had left her things. After toweling herself dry, she settled back in the chair and pulled a bottle of sunscreen out of her tote, slathering a generous amount of the fragranced cream onto her bare arms and shoulders. It was a Bronzed Babe lotion, she noted, turning the bottle over and eyeing the famous logo. She made a face. Whatever the marketing might have said, she didn't think much of the product. The artificial fragrance of pineapples was strong and cloying, and she felt like she was reeking of it from every pore.

"*WHATCHA' DOIN'?*" said Hemingway, who had flown over to join her and was now perched on the back of the lounge chair.

"Reapplying sunscreen," said Ellie, rubbing her arms vigorously and hoping that the smell of the cream would dissipate once it was absorbed.

"*WHATCHA' DOIN'?*" said the parrot again.

OK, this is getting a bit repetitive, Ellie grumbled silently. She was about to give an impatient answer when she realized that the parrot wasn't talking to her. He was watching a grey-haired woman in baggy harem pants and a loose cotton top, who was walking between the rows of lounge chairs and cabanas arranged around the pool. Ellie was surprised to see that it was Sandy O'Brien. She'd thought that the activist was still in custody, but the police had obviously released her.

"*WHATCHA' DOIN'?*" called Hemingway again, arching his neck and watching Sandy curiously.

Ellie's eyes widened as she saw what the woman *was* doing. She was moving furtively between the various seats and stopping every so often to bend down and stick a flyer into one of the beach totes and bags lying about. Most people were too busy with their families or friends to take much notice, and Sandy's slick, practiced movements showed that this was something she'd done many times before. She skirted around the back of Ellie's lounge chair and then—when she thought Ellie wasn't looking—she ducked down and quickly shoved a flyer into Ellie's beach bag.

"What are you doing?" Ellie demanded, twisting around.

"I'm educating you, dear," said Sandy with a superior smile. She looked Ellie up and down. "Do you know why you're wearing that bikini? Are you wearing it for yourself or is it because you think it'll make you look good to men?"

"I... it's none of your business!"

Sandy continued, undaunted: "You're doing it because you think it's the ideal of beauty. You're exposing your body because you think it's the only way to be considered attractive. That's the lie sold to all the young girls in our patriarchal society: that they have to prostitute themselves and degrade their bodies just to be noticed and valued."

"Choosing to wear a bikini doesn't mean that I'm degrading my body," said Ellie defensively.

Sandy shook her head sadly. "You poor thing...

you don't even realize how brainwashed you are."

Ellie flushed at the older woman's patronizing tone. "And have you been trying to 'educate' the bikini contest girls too?" she asked. She pulled the homemade flyer out of her bag and waved it in Sandy's face. "They found leaflets just like this one among their things in the changing room. You were up to your tricks in the spa yesterday morning, weren't you? Sneaking around and shoving unsolicited propaganda into people's personal belongings, just like you're doing now."

Sandy folded her arms. "So what if I was?"

"What do you mean, 'So what?'" said Ellie, almost spluttering with indignation. "You had no right to break into the place and spam people like that! It... it must be a form of trespassing or something!"

Sandy snorted. "Don't be ridiculous. Distributing information is hardly a crime. Anyway, it's a moot point since I wasn't there."

"Oh bollocks!" said Ellie, really starting to lose her temper. "Don't try to deny it! You were at the spa yesterday morning—I know you were! Who else would be sticking these flyers into the girls' things?"

"*OH BOLLOCKS!*" screeched Hemingway. "*OH BOLLOCKS!*"

Ellie shot the parrot an exasperated look, trying to ignore him as she turned back to Sandy. She narrowed her eyes at the other woman. "And maybe you didn't just stop at distributing flyers—maybe you decided to get a bit more hands-on."

Sandy's face hardened. "You're just like the police. They want to pin the murder on me too, but like I told them: I'm an activist, not a murderer. I had nothing to do with that poor girl's death! What do you think I am? I may have strong views, but I would never kill."

"You have a history of aggressive behavior at protest marches, though," Ellie pointed out.

"That's different! That's necessary force directed at authority members who try to oppress us, but I would never commit cold-blooded murder. Besides, why would I want to kill Brandi? I've dedicated my life to protecting vulnerable girls like her, to stop them from being exploited and, yes, even abused. You have no idea what happens at Don Palmer's so-called bikini contests. The man is an animal. If you're really looking for someone who's likely to harm one of the girls, you should be looking at him, not me!"

"*NOT ME!*" squawked Hemingway.

Ellie looked at the other woman scornfully. "Don Palmer? But he would have no reason to kill one of his own contestants. The last thing he needs is a murder investigation in the middle of his high-profile bikini pageant."

"That depends. It might be the lesser of two evils," said Sandy. "He might think it's worth it, to save his own skin."

Ellie frowned. "I don't understand what you mean."

Sandy raised her eyebrows. "You don't know? You

haven't heard the rumors? The gossip about Palmer's dirty reputation?"

Ellie shook her head. "What rumors?"

Sandy gave a disbelieving laugh. "Where have you been, honey?"

"*WHERE HAVE YOU BEEN, HONEY?*" echoed Hemingway.

"It's been going on for years," Sandy continued with a grim smile. "Girls accusing Palmer of sexual assault and indecent behavior, of abusing his position as a sponsor of the contest and taking advantage of them..."

Ellie thought suddenly of the day on the catamaran and Don Palmer's lecherous manner as he offered to put sunscreen on the girls' backs.

"Have you got any proof of this?" Ellie asked.

Sandy shrugged. "Oh, there have been several complaints and even accusations of assault and rape. But the girls never have proof and it becomes a case of 'he said, she said'... and in the end, he always pays them off. It's disgusting what money can buy you, especially when you've got an immoral lawyer. So Palmer has always managed to hush things up." She wagged a finger. "But your past always catches up with you in the end. Palmer won't be able to sweep things under the carpet forever and he knows it, so he's getting more and more desperate."

"But what does all this have to do with Brandi?"

Sandy gave her an impatient look. "Isn't it obvious? Palmer must have tried to grope her or something, and then tried to buy her silence. But maybe Brandi wouldn't play ball. Maybe she refused to be bought off and even threatened to expose him. If she had some kind of proof, that could be the end of him. Times are changing now, you know. Used to be that men like Don Palmer could get away with anything, but in today's environment, with the #MeToo movement... well, more powerful men than him have been arrested and imprisoned for sexual assault." She leaned forward to look Ellie straight in the eye. "If Palmer was faced with that, he could be willing to do anything to silence the girl—even murder."

CHAPTER THIRTEEN

The conversation with Sandy O'Brien left Ellie troubled. Long after the woman had left, Ellie remained sitting on her lounge chair, staring into space and frowning. Hemingway perched on the back of her chair, watching the other guests around them and whistling and calling out "OH BOLLOCKS!" every so often. But for once, Ellie barely noticed his antics. It wasn't until a sleek black shape jumped into her lap that she started out of her somber reverie.

"Oh, Mojito!" Ellie cried. "Ouch! Your claws!"

"*MIAOW!*" said the little black feline, looking up at Ellie with her big green eyes.

"*OUCH!*" croaked Hemingway. "*BAD KITTY! BAAAAD KITTY!*"

Mojito ignored the macaw. Instead, she began to make kneading motions with her front paws.

Ellie winced again. "Ow... oww... ow! That really hurts, Mojito," she complained, trying to shift the cat sideways so that Mojito's claws weren't digging into the skin of her bare thighs.

Her squirming knocked over the still-open bottle of Bronzed Babe sunscreen next to her, spilling a few drops of the cream onto the lounge chair. The pungent smell of pineapples filled the air again and Mojito drew back suddenly. The little black cat sneezed and then, with a hiss, jumped off the lounge chair and trotted away.

Ellie picked up the bottle and secured the cap again, thinking wryly that Mojito obviously shared her opinion of the sunscreen's overpowering perfume! She was just returning the bottle to her bag when she noticed a woman walking slowly past on the path next to them. Her face was strained, her brow was furrowed, and she looked like she was deep in thought—and not very pleasant thoughts either. But what really caught Ellie's attention was the fact that the woman looked vaguely familiar.

Do I know her? Where have I seen her before? mused Ellie, eyeing the woman and racking her brains. Then she remembered: *The spa! This is the beauty therapist who was looking after Brandi... Monica—yes, that's right! Monica.*

The last time Ellie had seen her, they had been standing in the treatment room together, staring down at Brandi's lifeless body. She wondered if the girl's murder was responsible for Monica's dark demeanor. Ellie was just debating whether to call out and say hello when Hemingway suddenly let out an unearthly screech and yelled:

"*WHERE HAVE YOU BEEN, HONEY?*"

It startled Monica so much that she tripped and stumbled sideways. Ellie sprang up and caught hold of the woman's arm, helping her regain her balance.

"Oh! God, that bird scared me," Monica cried, clutching a hand to her chest and scowling at Hemingway. Then she gave Ellie a grateful look. "Thanks. I would have fallen flat on my face if you hadn't caught me."

"That's OK. It's Monica, isn't it?" said Ellie with a friendly smile.

"Right, and you're—" Monica blinked as she suddenly recognized Ellie. "—oh! You're the girl who..." She trailed off awkwardly.

"Yeah, I found Brandi with you." Ellie glanced at the woman's uniform. "Are you back at work already? I would have thought that they'd let you have a few days off after what happened."

"The spa *is* still closed. The police have it taped off as a crime scene. But the resort also offers in-room treatments for guests and they're really popular, so some of us need to keep working. The spa manager did offer to give me time off but... well... I need the money," said Monica with a shrug. "No use sitting at home brooding. It's not like it's going to bring her back, right?"

"No, I suppose not. It must have been a horrible

shock for you, though," said Ellie sympathetically. "I mean, she was your client."

Monica shrugged again and looked down. "Yeah. I guess."

Ellie looked at her curiously. Was it her imagination or did the woman seem more guilty and uncomfortable than upset? She cleared her throat and said in a chatty voice:

"I'll bet you haven't been able to stop thinking about the murder—I wouldn't, if it were me! I'd be wondering if there was anything I'd missed yesterday morning, like maybe something I saw... or heard...?" She trailed off and looked hopefully at Monica, but the therapist didn't take the bait, so she continued: "I mean, did you notice Brandi acting strange at all?"

Monica shook her head. "No, like I told the police: she was totally fine when I left the room. I'd just put the warm towel on her face, so the steam could open up her pores, and she was lying on the bed all happy and comfortable."

"And she seemed completely normal?"

"Yeah... I mean, she was kinda drowsy and not saying much, but a lot of guests are like that at the spa. You know, they go there to chill out and relax, and we try not to talk to them too much if they don't seem to want to chat."

"And you said you left the room to get something?" said Ellie, recalling what the woman had told her when they bumped into each other in the corridor outside Brandi's room.

"Yes, I'd... uh... run out of... cotton swabs and I had to go to the store cupboard to get some more."

"Oh." Ellie was silent for a moment.

She could have sworn that she had seen cotton swabs in Brandi's room. She could still see the room in her mind's eye, with the soothing beachy décor and the long counter along one wall with the row of glass dispenser jars on top. It had been a hurried glance but she was sure she'd seen cotton swabs in one of the jars, next to the facial sponges, gauze pads, cosmetic wipes, emery boards, and other items. So did that mean that Monica was lying about the reason she'd left the room?

Ellie looked up to see the other woman watching her tensely. She gave her a bright smile and said: "Sorry, I was confused for a moment when you said that, because I was just remembering back to yesterday morning and I thought I *did* see a jar with cotton swabs in it when I went into the room."

Ellie tried not to sound accusing, but she could see Monica flushing nevertheless.

"Yeah, I... uh... must have missed seeing that," the beauty therapist said quickly. "There are so many jars on the counters—I must have looked real quick and didn't check enough."

"*OH BOLLOCKS!*" said Hemingway.

Ellie hid a grin. For once, the parrot was voicing her thoughts. Aloud, though, she murmured, "Oh, yes, of course. Erm... so have you been working at the resort spa long?"

"A few years," said Monica. "Why?"

"Oh, I was just curious. Is it very different to working at a day spa in the city?"

"A little, I guess. Like, if you work downtown, you might get locals who become regulars, whereas at the resort, you're pretty much getting new clients all the time. But you get to meet more international guests too; you know, people from different backgrounds and stuff, which is pretty cool."

"Yes, that must keep your job interesting! Although I suppose at a luxury resort like this, you might also get some wealthy customers who make difficult demands sometimes—"

Monica stiffened suddenly. "I don't know what you mean," she snapped. "None of my clients have ever asked for anything inappropriate."

"Oh... I didn't mean to imply anything," said Ellie, taken aback. She had just been making random conversation while her mind was still mulling over the cotton swabs, and she was surprised by the other woman's defensive reaction.

Monica must have realized that her response was unnecessarily aggressive because she quickly forced a smile and said in a conciliatory tone, "Sorry, I'm... uh... a bit tired. Haven't been sleeping too well." She glanced at the watch on her wrist. "Anyway, I'd better get going, otherwise I'll be late for my next appointment. Nice talking to you."

Ellie watched the woman walk away and mused out loud: "I don't know why but I have a feeling that you're a liar, Monica."

"LIAR!" croaked a voice behind her.

Ellie turned back to grin at Hemingway, still perched on her lounge chair. "Yeah, Hemingway... Liar, liar, pants on fire—have you heard that one?"

"*LIAR! PANTS ON!*"

Ellie giggled. "No, you have to say the whole phrase together: *Liar, liar, pants on fire!*"

Hemingway cocked his head and eyed her brightly. Ellie repeated the phrase and the parrot flapped his wings excitedly.

"*FIRE!*" he screeched.

Ellie groaned. *Oh no, what have I done?*

"No, no, for God's sake, Hemingway, don't start shouting that! You'll cause mass panic at the resort," she said quickly. "OK, forget that. How about we teach you a nice British phrase? Say: 'Fancy a cuppa?'"

"*CUPPA?*"

"Yes, fancy a cuppa?"

"*FANCY CUPPA?*"

Ellie chuckled. "We'll work on it."

CHAPTER FOURTEEN

The sky was streaked in multi-colored hues from the light of the setting sun as Ellie followed Blake across the marina later that evening. He led her toward a ramshackle wooden shack that was perched on stilts, right at the end of the main boardwalk. She eyed the structure doubtfully as they approached. It looked weather-beaten and dilapidated, with old fishing nets and rusty license plates hanging from the walls, and an ancient wooden mermaid figurehead hanging above the door, next to a crooked sign which read: "*THE HUNKY DORY FISH SHACK.*"

Inside, the rustic ambience continued, with plywood floors, old newspapers covering the tables, and customers all noisily using mallets to crack open their stone crabs. Pieces of cracked shell were flying in all directions, scattering all over the floor, where they seemed to join piles of other old cracked shells.

Blake laughed as he saw her expression and said: "That's a unique quirk of this place. You know the famous Raffles Bar in Singapore where it's tradition to throw the empty shells of peanuts on the floor? Well, this is the local seafood version."

"Are you sure it's just empty shells on the floor? I could have sworn I saw a live crab scuttling sideways just now," said Ellie, looking nervously around.

Blake laughed again and said, "Hey, I know this place doesn't look like much, but I promise, it serves the best seafood in Tampa Bay. Well, in my opinion anyway."

"As long as it remains standing," muttered Ellie under her breath as she followed him to a table on the rickety outdoor deck.

They sat down at a table right at the edge of the deck, by the wooden railing which looked out over the calm water of the Intracoastal Waterway, and Ellie had to admit that the setting was gorgeous. The water view was soothing, there was a taste of salt in the breeze that gently stirred her hair, and a wonderful mouthwatering smell of hot food wafted from the kitchen.

"I've wanted to bring you to this place for a while," said Blake enthusiastically. "I mean, the seafood at the resort is great—don't get me wrong—but nothing beats the authentic experience of a traditional Florida 'fish shack.' The surroundings might not be too fancy, but I think the atmosphere more than makes up for it."

"I know what you mean," agreed Ellie. "It's the same back in England. Like historic pubs, you know, which might not be as posh as the big hotels or country clubs, but you just can't replicate the experience of having a pint there in front of a roaring fire, while tucking into some traditional British foods like Yorkshire pudding or fish 'n' chips."

"Exactly!" said Blake. Then he glanced at the large blackboard propped up against the wall of the restaurant and added, "Well, you might not be able to get your beloved fish 'n' chips here, but I think you'll find the grouper sandwich just as good."

"It's a white fish, isn't it?" said Ellie, frowning. "I feel like I've heard of it but I don't really know what it looks like."

"It's not a very attractive fish," said Blake, chuckling. "It's got bugged-out eyes and a big, ugly brown body. You can go fishing for these guys off the coast and, man, you won't believe how big they can get. The Atlantic goliath grouper can get to, like, eight hundred pounds! But the flesh is incredibly tender when cooked and it's really tasty. You can have it cooked all sorts of ways, of course, but the Florida specialty is a grouper sandwich."

"Oh, you mean like the Cuban sandwich?" said Ellie. "It's a famous local food?"

"Yeah, kind of, although there's more variation with grouper sandwiches. You can get them fried, grilled, or blackened Cajun-style, and there's like a million different toppings and condiments you can put on them. Every restaurant has its signature style. My favorite is one of the options on the menu here: deep-fried in beer batter, in a brioche bun with lettuce, tomato, and onion, and Thousand Island dressing." Blake smacked his lips. "*Sooo* good."

"OK, you've convinced me," said Ellie with a chuckle. "I'm going to have that. I'm not even going to bother looking at the rest of the menu."

"And how about we have some stone crab to start?" Blake suggested. "It's a good time to eat them. They're in season from October to May."

"Oh, yes, they're delicious! I had some at the resort, on the night of the awards dinner for the Key Lime Pie contest. Sol showed me how to eat them."

Blake grinned and leaned forward, saying in a mock undertone, "Well, don't tell Sol, but I think the stone crabs here are even better. Plus, they don't pre-crack them here, like they do at the resort restaurants. I always think they taste better when you crack them fresh yourself and, as a doctor, I highly recommend a session with that mallet for getting any frustrations out of your system!"

Ellie laughed and, when a large plate of stone crab claws, together with a wooden mallet, was brought to their table a short while later, she reached for the mallet with gusto. Blake put his hand out at the same time and they ended up in a slight tug-of-war.

"If they're too hard, of course, I can crack them for

you," he offered.

"No, I can manage," Ellie insisted, pulling the mallet toward her. She gave Blake a teasing look. "And you're lucky that Sandy O'Brien wasn't here to hear you say that. She'd probably flay you alive for daring to imply that I—a woman—am not up to the task."

Blake rolled his eyes. "For the record, I don't think chivalry and feminism are mutually exclusive."

"I'm teasing," said Ellie, grinning. "And maybe I'm being unfair to Sandy. It's just that she seems so hardcore, I imagine she'd be the type of feminist who would object to men holding doors for her and stuff like that. It seems a bit silly, really. I mean, back home, that would just be seen as good manners."

"Same here in America," said Blake. "My mother always brought me up to treat ladies well—that doesn't mean I don't respect them as equals."

"I don't think women like Sandy really do feminism any favors," said Ellie dryly. She made a face. "Aunt Olive really likes her, but I have to say, I find her quite off-putting. I can see why the police have her in their sights, especially given her record. I mean, I do agree with Sandy's sentiments about the exploitation of women, but… but she's so aggressive and judgmental! And so volatile too! I wouldn't be surprised if she *did* have something to do with Brandi's murder." She sighed. "The problem is, Aunt Olive is absolutely convinced that Sandy is innocent and she's determined to prove it. Or rather, she wants *me* to prove it," she added. "Except that I'm not sure I want to play detective this time."

"Well, I've been doing a bit of sleuthing on my own," Blake said with a smug look.

Ellie looked at him in surprise. "Really?"

Blake nodded. "I think the police might be missing something about the method of murder."

"What d'you mean?"

"The official line is that Brandi was suffocated by someone using one of the large cushions in the treatment room—and that's true. She was. But I don't think that was the only thing the murderer used."

"You mean, another weapon? But there were no other marks or signs of injury on her," protested Ellie.

"No, not another weapon exactly. I think Brandi was drugged first. I spoke to the ME and he agreed with me." Blake leaned forward earnestly. "Do you realize how difficult it is to smother someone with a pillow? It's not like how they make it look in the movies. Maybe if you're really old and weak, or sick and frail, then yes, someone could smother you just by pressing something down on your face. But for most healthy adults, the survival reflex would make them fight and thrash like crazy. Unless you tied them down or put their head in a vice or something, you wouldn't be able to easily hold them still long enough to kill them. Don't forget, people can hold their breath for short periods—you'd need to cut off their air supply for a sufficient length of time for someone to suffocate."

Ellie thought back to the pristine condition of Brandi's room when she had walked into it yesterday morning. "Yeah, Brandi's room was really neat. In fact, I didn't even think that anything could be wrong until I walked around the treatment bed and saw her face…" Ellie shuddered at the memory.

"Exactly," said Blake. "That's what I thought when I walked in. If someone had tried to smother her, surely she would have struggled and fought back? There would have been things knocked over, towels kicked around, maybe even the bed bumped out of its normal position… but there were none of those things."

"Did you tell the police?"

Blake nodded. "Like I said, I discussed it with the ME, who agrees with me and is going to confirm things from his end, via the tox screen. But that's going to take a day or two to come back. I also raised it with Detective Carson. He was a bit dismissive, though—he thinks that Brandi was probably just very relaxed or even asleep on the bed and the murderer took her by surprise."

"Couldn't that be true?" asked Ellie.

"Yes, it could, but even if that had happened, she would still have fought back once she woke up and found that someone was trying to suffocate her. No matter how relaxed you are, your survival instinct kicks in," said Blake. He leaned back. "Anyway, we'll see when we get the full autopsy report. If I'm right, the toxicology analysis should find traces of some kind of sedative in Brandi's system. And while I'm waiting for the results, I thought I might as well do some investigating of my own. I've been talking to some of the resort staff, trying to get an idea of the girls' movements that morning and when someone might have had the opportunity to drug Brandi."

"You think it had to have been done that morning?"

"Yes, although the time depends on what drug was used. It either had to be something fast-acting, like chloroform—in which case, it was probably administered to her in the room right before she was attacked—or it was something that had a longer time to take effect, in which case it could have been given to her earlier that morning." He glanced at Ellie. "You didn't smell anything strange when you walked into Brandi's room, did you? Chloroform has a distinctive sweet odor."

Ellie struggled to remember. "I don't think so, although there are so many fragrances in a spa—you know, like lavender and plumeria and stuff—it might mask other odors."

"Yes, and in any case, chloroform is pretty volatile so it might not linger in the air for long," said Blake.

"Couldn't something have been given to her the night before?" asked Ellie.

"I doubt it. Most drugs would have worn off by the next morning. However, there *are* certain over-the-counter medications known to cause delayed drowsiness and sedation, so Brandi could have been given something earlier that morning, which wouldn't have taken effect until she was at the spa."

"Like what?"

"Oh, like certain antihistamines. Benadryl is a famous example. It's a common cold medicine and antihistamine here in the U.S., and it can be bought in drugstores without a prescription. But it contains diphenhydramine, which has some pretty potent side effects in large doses or if mixed with alcohol—such as low blood pressure, rapid heart rate, seizures, tremors, nausea, and vomiting. But most importantly, in this case, it can cause extreme drowsiness or even cause you to pass out."

"Wow! I'm surprised you can buy this drug without a prescription!" said Ellie.

"Well, death from diphenhydramine overdose is very rare—although you *can* get serious cardiac arrhythmias, which can be fatal," Blake admitted. "In any case, Brandi didn't die from the poisoning itself; she was definitely suffocated. All the external evidence—the bloodshot eyes and bruising around the nose and mouth—point to that. However, I think drugs played an indirect role in her murder by making her too weak or sedated to fight back."

CHAPTER FIFTEEN

They were interrupted by a waitress bringing their main order, and Ellie was silent as she tasted her grouper sandwich.

"Well?" asked Blake, his brown eyes keen.

"Mm... delicious," mumbled Ellie with her mouth full. She swallowed and beamed at him. "It's really good! So tender and flaky on the inside, but crispy on the outside... and I love the tangy Thousand Island sauce." She took another bite. "It's lived up to all your hype!"

Blake grinned, looking pleased. They ate in silence for a few minutes, then Ellie said, unable to resist returning to the mystery:

"So if Brandi was drugged first, that means finding out who could have done it could also point to her killer."

"Yes. It would have to be someone who was around her and had ample opportunity—at breakfast that morning, maybe."

"I was at breakfast with the girls," said Ellie.

"Did you notice anything?" asked Blake.

Ellie shook her head. "The only thing I noticed was that Brandi seemed a bit subdued. You know, she was normally always the 'life and soul of the party,' but that morning she seemed very quiet. But the other girls told me that Brandi had overindulged with the cocktails at the lobby bar the night before, so I thought maybe she was just a bit hungover." She glanced at Blake. "Oh my God—do you think she was showing the effects of the drug already?"

Blake shrugged. "I don't know. Maybe. Or she could really have been hungover. Do you remember who was sitting next to her?"

Ellie furrowed her brow. "I remember Amber being on one side of her, because I remember seeing her try to provoke Brandi... and I think Kimberley might have been on the other side? Or maybe it was Roxy. Sorry, I can't really remember."

"That's OK. If you were all sitting pretty close together at a small table, it could have been any of the girls, since anyone could have easily reached across and put something in Brandi's food or drink when nobody was watching."

"Yes, and it was a buffet too," said Ellie. "So people kept getting up and sitting down and walking back and forth... plus I remember a couple of the girls swapped seats midway through, so there was a lot of confusion and moving around. Of course, the most likely person is—" She broke off.

Blake looked at her enquiringly. "Yes?"

"Nothing. It was just a thought. I'm probably wrong," said Ellie quickly. The conversation with her sister had dented her confidence, and now she said sheepishly: "I'm not a detective or any kind of professional investigator, and I probably shouldn't be speculating."

"No, but you have good instincts," said Blake. "And you've been right before, when the police have gotten it wrong. I would back you over Detective Carson any day."

"Oh." Ellie flushed with pleasure, feeling her confidence rise again at Blake's words. "Thanks."

"So?" Blake raised an eyebrow and smiled encouragingly at her.

Ellie took a deep breath: "Well, the obvious suspect is Amber. She was next door in the spa and she had direct access to Brandi's room via a connecting door. Plus, there was a bit of... erm... 'bad blood' between Brandi and Amber. The other contestants were telling me about it at the Snack Shack last night: the two girls hated each other. They were the top contenders to win the contest, you know, so I suppose a lot of it was jealous rivalry. Apparently, there had been several catfights between them already. In fact, they had a huge fight the night before and Amber was overhead muttering threats under her breath."

Blake looked thoughtful. "Jealous rivalry seems like a far-fetched motive for murder, but I suppose if emotions were running high..."

"The other girls think it might have been an accident—like maybe Amber only meant to scare Brandi and 'teach her a lesson,' as they say, but things got out of hand and it ended badly."

"No," said Blake, shaking his head firmly. "If I'm right—and I'm pretty sure I am—and Brandi was drugged first, that means it wasn't an impulsive act of revenge. It was cold-blooded, premeditated murder."

Ellie thought back to the previous morning. "The only thing is, Amber reacted like the other girls when she rushed in and saw Brandi," she said. "I mean, her shock seemed genuine."

"She could be a good actress," said Blake. "If she's cool enough to plan a murder, she'd be cool enough to put on an act."

"I suppose..." Ellie bit her lip. "Look, I know Amber's the logical suspect, but are we just jumping on her because she's the easy, obvious choice?"

Blake raised his eyebrows. "Why not? Most of the time, the most obvious answer *is* the right answer. From what I understand, Amber was also the only girl who was alone at the time. Her technician had to go out to get a new eye pillow because Amber complained that it smelled funny, so she was conveniently left alone in her room." Seeing Ellie's skeptical expression, he added: "OK, who else do you suspect? Other than your technician, who the receptionist vouched for, all the other technicians gave statements that they were in their rooms with their clients, so they and the other girls all had alibis for the time of the murder."

Ellie hesitated, then she voiced the niggling thought that had been at the back of her mind.

"There's also Gina."

Blake's brows drew together. "Gina?"

"Yes. She didn't have a treatment—she opted to just go into the steam room. So that means she didn't have anyone with her."

Blake looked at her, frowning. "Why should that matter?"

Ellie hesitated again, not liking his defensive tone. Instead of answering directly, she said: "I saw Gina when I stepped out of my own room: she was just *returning* to the steam room, so she wasn't inside there the whole time."

"Yes, I know. She told me—and Detective Carson—that she'd gone out briefly to the restroom at the end of the corridor."

"But she can't have!" Ellie burst out. "I went into the restroom too, straight after I saw her, because I was searching for Mojito and I thought the cat might have gone in there. Anyway, there was a huge puddle from the leak at one of the sinks. It had literally spread over the entire floor."

Blake looked at her quizzically. "So? I still don't

understand what you're getting at, Ellie."

"So anyone who had gone to the restroom must have stepped in that puddle," said Ellie. "And they would have tracked wet footprints across the carpet in the corridor when they came back out again. I know because I did." She paused, then added in a carefully neutral voice: "But Gina didn't."

"Are you saying what I think you're saying? Are you suggesting that Gina might be the *murderer*?"

"I..." Ellie hesitated, then she raised her chin and met Blake's eyes. "Yes, I am."

Blake made a sound of disgust. "That's the dumbest idea I've ever heard in my life!"

Ellie flushed. "Why? It's a perfectly reasonable conclusion."

"It's not reasonable at all!" said Blake. "It's a stupid suggestion."

"It's not stupid at all!" retorted Ellie. "It makes perfect sense, actually. Gina had obviously lied about where she had gone. Why would she have done that, unless she had something to hide?"

"It's crazy to suggest that Gina might be the murderer," insisted Blake. "For one thing, what motive could she have?"

Ellie thought back to the conversation she had overheard between Gina and Don Palmer on the catamaran and once again heard the blonde woman's smooth voice in her head:

"This is going to be the most talked-about bikini contest in Florida for a long time to come... I've got

stuff in motion that's going to generate publicity like you've never seen before... I'm known as the best in the business, because I get results—no matter what it takes."

"Maybe she wanted to do something that would get the contest into the news," Ellie said.

"A publicity stunt?" said Blake incredulously. "You're kidding, right? You're suggesting that Gina might have committed murder just to get PR for the contest?"

"Any publicity is good publicity. I heard Gina say that herself. I also heard her promise Don Palmer to do whatever it takes to make this the most talked-about contest in Florida. Well, judging by the headlines I saw today, it's happening."

Blake sat back, leaving the rest of his grouper sandwich uneaten, and made an angry gesture. "I can't believe you'd even think like that, Ellie."

Ellie gritted her teeth. Blake's defensive attitude was really beginning to annoy her. "If this was anyone else, you wouldn't have a problem with my thinking. It's only because it's Gina."

"That's not true."

"Yes, it is! The facts show that she lied about her alibi, which means that she could be a likely suspect. Why can't you accept that?" asked Ellie in frustration.

"Because I know Gina! We dated for several years, we've been on vacation together, I've spent hours and hours with her—"

"Maybe you don't know her as well as you think," Ellie snapped, thinking of the night before and the way Gina had changed as soon as Blake was around.

"What's that supposed to mean?"

"I mean, maybe Gina puts on a different face when she's with you," said Ellie bluntly. "But there's a side to her that you don't really know. After all, you said yourself that Amber could be putting on an act. So why not Gina?"

"That's... that's different," argued Blake.

"There! You see? You're being completely biased!"

"If anyone is being biased, it's you. You're prejudiced against Gina because you're jealous."

"What? Jealous? *Me?*" cried Ellie, her voice becoming shrill with outrage.

"I know you're not comfortable with her being here and I'm sorry about that," said Blake impatiently. "But I can't just turn on her because you don't like her. Gina and I have a history and I still care about her, as a friend. I can't abandon her, especially now that she's facing a tough situation, just because you can't deal with it."

"I never said you should!" said Ellie indignantly. "All I'm saying is that she was obviously not being truthful about her movements on the morning of the murder and you can't rule her out as a suspect!"

They stared at each other across the table, breathing hard. Ellie was furious that their date, which had been going so well, had descended into a sordid fight... and it was all because of Gina Ross!

Maybe Blake read her mind, because he took a deep breath and let it out slowly. Then he passed a hand over his face and gave Ellie a rueful smile.

"I'm sorry. The last thing I wanted for our evening together was to be fighting over Gina. Look, can we just... change the subject?"

Ellie took a deep breath as well, feeling mollified by Blake's attempt at an apology. She gave him a half-hearted smile. "I'm sorry too." She took another deep breath, looking around and casting for another topic. "Erm... so... how did you find this place?"

For the rest of the meal, they made small talk, careful to steer clear of the topics of Gina, the bikini contest, and the murder. By the time they'd finished and were walking out of the restaurant, the previous atmosphere of easy camaraderie was somewhat restored. Ellie found her mood lifting even further when Blake took her to a local ice cream parlor for dessert—a tiny place crammed full of beloved old-school candy, like Pop Rocks, peppermint puffs, and retro candy necklaces, and serving a selection of traditional milkshakes and ice cream flavors. Clutching their ice creams, they strolled across to the nearby beach marina and walked slowly out to the end of the pier. The night was balmy, with a light breeze that brought with it the smell of the ocean, and Ellie sighed with contentment as she watched the lights shimmering out on the water. By the time she managed to consume her towering waffle cone of butterscotch-dipped, soft-serve ice cream, garnished with homemade fudge brownies and fresh strawberries, she was feeling warm and fuzzy, and ready to forgive anyone anything.

So as Blake walked her to the front door of her villa suite, back at the resort, she turned to him with a big smile and said:

"Thank you for a lovely evening. No, really, I had a brilliant time."

"I'm glad," said Blake, smiling. "I had a great time too."

He paused as they stopped outside the villa door. Then he took a step closer. Ellie felt her heart begin that familiar deep thumping in her chest. She tilted her head to look up at him and caught her breath at the expression in his brown eyes. Was Blake going to kiss her at last? She had been dreaming of this moment since that first day when they'd met on the beach. Oh, Blake had given her a few quick pecks on previous dates, but they had never had "the kiss." Now, Ellie stared up at him, terrified and yet thrilled at the same time.

Slowly, Blake leaned forward and, after a second's hesitation, Ellie rose up on tiptoes to meet him halfway. His arms slid around her, pulling her gently to him, and then Ellie felt the touch of his lips, warm and firm on hers. Her senses filled with the clean masculine scent of him, the feel of his hair, thick and springy beneath her fingers, and the hard length of his body molded against hers...

"Blake! BLAKE!"

They broke apart and Ellie turned in disbelief to see Gina rushing up the walkway toward them.

I don't believe this! she fumed. She was just about to open her mouth and deliver a blistering putdown to the other woman when Gina's next words stopped her in her tracks:

"Come quick! There's been another attack on one of the girls!"

CHAPTER SIXTEEN

Ellie followed Blake and Gina as they hurried toward the wing where the bikini contestants' rooms were located. When they entered the building, they could hear a general hubbub of voices, shrill and scared, and as they rounded the corner, Ellie saw a group of people congregating outside the open door of a room at the end of the corridor. Several members of the resort staff, as well as a man in a resort security uniform, were hovering outside the door and, when they shouldered their way in, they found the room crammed full of the girls. They were milling around the twin beds in the center of the room, talking and gesticulating in great agitation. The only one who stood apart was Amber, who was on her own by the windows, her arms crossed and her face scowling.

At first glance, Ellie was relieved to see no dead bodies or even any injuries in sight. She did see Roxy sitting huddled on one of the twin beds, though. The girl looked distraught: her face was red and blotchy, her eyes wide and scared, and she was wailing and gasping. An older lady in a Housekeeping uniform was patting the girl's shoulder and trying to comfort Roxy, and she looked up with relief when Blake entered the room.

Quickly, she rose to let him have access to the bedside, saying: "Oh, Doctor! She's hysterical and I can't calm her down!"

Blake sat down beside Roxy and gently reached out to grasp her wrist. He checked her pulse while talking to her in a low, calm voice. Ellie stood awkwardly next to him, wanting to help but not knowing what to do.

"I can't... I can't...!" gasped Roxy, hyperventilating. "Oh my God, I'm going to suffocate... just like Brandi!"

"No, you're not," said Blake, his voice firm but calm. "Look at me, Roxy! Focus on my voice. Good. Now—listen to me: take a breath in through your nose and then let it out—slowly—don't rush it—just nice and easy... Good... In... Out... In... Out..."

"What about breathing into a paper bag?" asked Gina. "They do that for panic attacks on all the TV shows."

"It's not advised anymore," said Blake tersely. "It's not very effective and can be dangerous if carbon dioxide levels rise too high, especially if you have certain medical conditions. Staying calm and breathing slowly and deliberately is just as effective. In any case, her pulse seems normal..." He frowned slightly, then turned back to Roxy, who seemed to finally be calming down. She took a long, shuddering breath and sat up straighter, saying in a shaky voice:

"I'm... I'm feeling better."

"What happened?" asked Ellie tentatively.

Roxy pointed a trembling finger at the head of her bed. There was a small carryall beside her pillow, with its zipper undone and clothes bursting out. Propped in the midst of the pile of clothes was a Barbie doll. But as Ellie stepped over to take a closer look, she felt a chill run up her spine. The doll's head had been yanked viciously off and lay upside down next to the body. And as if the sight of the headless doll wasn't disturbing enough, there was a crumpled piece of paper next to it with something scrawled across the surface in lurid pink. Ellie's eyes widened as she read the words: "*YOU'LL BE NEXT.*"

"It... it was there, waiting for me, when I got back to the room," said Roxy in a quavering voice. "It's... it's a warning, isn't it? Omigod, it's the killer—the one who murdered Brandi! I'm going to be the next to die!"

She looked as if she was going to dissolve into hysterics again, and it took Blake several more moments to calm her down. Ellie glanced at Gina, who had an inscrutable expression on her face.

"Have you called the police?" Ellie asked.

"Of course," snapped Gina. "They're on their way. But since no one was actually hurt, it's not exactly an emergency, is it?"

"You acted like it was urgent enough when you came to get Blake," muttered Ellie.

"That's because he's the resort doctor and Roxy was having a panic attack!" said Gina. "Anyway, it's probably just some stupid prank."

Roxy jerked her head up. "It's not a prank! It's a threat—a death threat!" she cried. "They thought it was just Brandi, but they're wrong! There's... there's like some psycho stalking all of us girls!"

The other contestants began chiming in, adding their own wild theories.

"Omigod, do you think it's a serial killer?"

"No, it's a hex! I told you there's a hex on the contest!"

"Maybe it's, like, some ex-beauty queen who has a grudge?"

"Or maybe it's someone who wants to get rid of the competition..."

The girls threw a dark look in Amber's direction. She was still holding herself aloof on the other side of the room, refusing to join in the general hubbub, but Ellie could see that Amber had heard the last remark. Her eyes flashed and she looked as if she was going to say something, but then she turned her head away and stared out the window instead.

"There's no hex on the contest," said Gina loudly.

"And there's no serial killer. Let's not overreact, OK? It *could* have just been a stupid prank. I mean, look at this! It's written using lipstick or something, like one of those scented glitter lipsticks. That's more like something a teenage kid messing around might use..." She picked up the note and waved it to show everyone. A strong artificial smell of raspberry wafted from the piece of paper.

"You shouldn't touch that," said Ellie quickly. "You could be contaminating evidence."

"Ellie's right," said Blake. "Now you've got your prints all over it and you could have muddled any fingerprints that the perpetrator might have left on the note."

Gina scowled and dropped the note back next to the doll. "Anyway, my point is, it's much more likely to be some teenager playing a prank than a serious criminal."

"But how did they get in my room?" asked Roxy. "I mean, there was nothing here when I was leaving to go down for dinner earlier. And no one else has a key, except Amber, but she went down before me and she didn't return until we came back together—right, Amber?" Roxy turned to her roommate.

"Right," said Amber.

"And was any of *your* stuff disturbed?" asked Ellie.

"No," said Amber shortly.

"Are you sure?"

Amber rolled her eyes. "Yeah, I keep my stuff neat, not like Roxy. I'd notice immediately if something had been moved." She gestured to the twin bed on the other side of the room, and Ellie saw that she was right. Unlike the mess on Roxy's side, the clothes there were folded in neat piles, shoes stored in special holders and arranged in rows, and the items on the bedside table were perfectly aligned, with identical spaces between them.

"What about the door?" asked Ellie. "Was it definitely shut when you girls came back? You know sometimes how latches don't fully click into place? Or did you notice if anyone had tampered with the lock or the handle?"

"I... I wasn't really paying much attention," Roxy mumbled.

Amber just shrugged, but it was obvious she hadn't looked closely either.

"We're not all trying to be Nancy Drew all the time, you know," said Gina sarcastically.

Ellie flushed and bit back the sharp retort that sprang to her lips.

Blake cleared his throat in the strained silence that followed and said: "How do you feel now, Roxy?"

"Better," said the girl. Then she asked timidly: "Can I have a glass of water?"

"I'll get it," said Ellie.

She went into the bathroom and picked up the glass beside the sink, then ran the cold water for a few minutes before filling it. As she was doing this, she glanced idly around and noted that the two groups of toiletries on either side of the vanity mirrored the room outside. One side was obviously Roxy's, with make-up items haphazardly piled into a small zip bag, bottles left uncapped, and used cotton buds littering the area. The other side was clearly Amber's, with creams and lotions arranged in rows according to height, make-up neatly stored in a plastic case, and nail file, razor, tweezers, and other tools lined up like a surgeon's instrument tray.

Then Ellie's gaze sharpened as she spied a small pouch tucked beside Amber's make-up case. It was partially open and she could see various boxes and tubes inside: an insect bite ointment, a packet of Tylenol, some bandages, a tube of post-sun aloe vera gel... and a small, flat box with the word "BENADRYL" clearly printed across its surface.

Ellie caught her breath. Throwing a glance over her shoulder to make sure that no one else had come into the bathroom, she reached into the pouch and pulled out the slim box. It was a packet of antihistamine tablets marketed as "quick dissolve."

Ellie stared down at it, frowning. The box felt fairly light and, when she opened it, she found only a couple of tablets left. A large dose had obviously been used up.

"What are you doing?"

Ellie jumped and turned around to find herself facing Amber. The girl was watching her with narrowed eyes.

"Oh! I... erm..." Ellie hastily shoved the Benadryl box back into the pouch and gave Amber a breezy smile. "I... I was just curious to see whether you had the same kinds of medicines in America as we do in the U.K. You know, like you call it Tylenol whereas we have Panadol, but they're both the same drug." She hesitated, then added boldly: "So... do you suffer from allergies, then?"

Amber glanced at the box in the open pouch. "Yeah. Sometimes. I get hives if I have too much shellfish."

"Oh... and do you think Benadryl is the best thing to take?" Ellie persisted. "I... erm... have a friend who suffers from allergies and she's always struggling to find a good antihistamine."

Amber shrugged. "It's OK, I guess. I don't normally take it, 'cos it can make you drowsy. But I ran out of my own stuff, so Gina gave me this from her stash."

Gina! Ellie stared at the other girl. "Gina gave you this?"

Before Amber could answer, Gina herself suddenly stuck her head into the bathroom. She eyed the two of them suspiciously.

"I thought you were getting water for Roxy," she said in an accusing tone.

"I was," said Ellie, holding up the glass of water.

Amber made a face. "Ugh. You don't wanna drink tap water—it tastes funky."

"You mean it's not safe to drink?" asked Ellie. "Back in England, I just drink water from the tap."

"Oh, it's safe in Florida too," said Gina briskly.

"Some people just don't like the taste."

"Yeah, I always drink bottled if I can," said Amber.

"There's some bottled water by the coffee machine outside," added Gina.

"Oh, yes, of course. I'd forgotten," said Ellie. She emptied the glass and hurriedly returned to the room, conscious of Gina still watching her. As she retrieved a bottle of water from the counter beside the mini-bar and took it over to Roxy, Ellie mulled over the little episode in the bathroom.

Was it just a coincidence that Amber had a packet of the very same drug likely administered to drug Brandi, and that a large amount of the tablets had been used up...?

Probably enough to sedate Brandi and make it easier to smother her, thought Ellie.

Amber had good reasons for hating Brandi and wanting her out of the picture. After all, the two girls had already had a history of conflict, and there was strong rivalry between them. By killing Brandi, Amber would have not only removed her main rival in the contest, but also gotten rid of a thorn in her side. And she'd had easy access to the murdered girl during the spa treatments through the connecting door between their rooms. With her beauty therapist popping out of her room, no one could vouch that she had remained in her own room the entire time so, effectively, she had no alibi.

But what about Gina? Was it an even greater coincidence that the packet of antihistamines had originally come from her? She might not have had any personal issues with Brandi, but she could have had an equally strong motive to kill her. After all, murder got you into all the headlines, and for someone who believed that "any publicity was good publicity," sacrificing one girl might have seemed a small price to pay for the greater reward of public hype and media attention. Could someone really be that ruthless, though? To commit murder just to get PR?

Ellie glanced thoughtfully across the room at the two women. Amber had returned to her moody contemplation by the window whilst Gina was hovering around Blake and Roxy. Either woman could have murdered Brandi. The question was: who had done it and why?

CHAPTER SEVENTEEN

It was nearly midnight by the time Ellie finally returned to her villa and she was expecting Aunt Olive to be in bed, but her aunt sprang up from the couch as soon as Ellie came in, and exclaimed:

"Great gibbons, Ellie—I've been waiting for you to come back for ages!"

Ellie eyed her aunt warily. She had a bad feeling that Aunt Olive was going to behave as usual and demand a blow-by-blow account of her date with Blake, including pumping her for intimate details of any sexy encounters. But to her surprise, instead of asking whether Blake was a good kisser, Aunt Olive said:

"Guess what, poppet—I've got proof that Don Palmer is the murderer!"

"*What?*"

Aunt Olive nodded eagerly. "I knew Sandy couldn't be guilty! She's being used as the scapegoat, just like I said. The real killer is Palmer—even if he didn't do the deed himself."

"What?" said Ellie again, really confused now. "What do you mean, he didn't do it himself? How can he be the killer if he didn't do it?"

"Well!" Aunt Olive's eyes sparkled. "Listen to this: after dinner, I decided to go for a short stroll instead of coming straight back to the villa. There's a walkway that loops around the big lawn beside the beach and it passes right by one of the wings which houses the beachfront suites. Guess who I saw leaving the last suite at the end of the block? Monica!"

"Monica—? Oh, the beauty therapist from the resort spa," said Ellie, remembering the woman she had met by the pool earlier that day.

"Yes. Lovely girl. She's done several facials for me. Anyway, she was creeping out of the French doors of the suite onto the private terrace and looking very furtive. It put my nostrils on instant high alert," declared Aunt Olive. "So I ducked behind a bush and waited to see what would happen. A second later, a man stuck his head out of the French door: it was Don Palmer!"

Ellie looked at her aunt quizzically. "And? I don't get it—what does it matter if you saw Monica leaving Palmer's suite? Maybe she'd gone over to give him an in-room massage. I met her by the pool earlier and she told me that Sunset Palms offers its guests the option to have treatments in their rooms. In fact, she was just on her way to an appointment when I saw her."

"Ahh, but I haven't told you what I heard them say!" said Aunt Olive, looking like a cat who had not only got the canary but the full-fat whipped cream with catnip sprinkles as well. "Palmer beckoned Monica back and said: *'Don't forget: what happened at the spa stays between us, huh?'* And Monica looked very uneasy as she said: *'Sure, Mr. Palmer.'* And then he smirked and said: *'Call me Don—after all, we're partners in crime now, right? So it's time to get a bit more personal, don't you think?'* And Monica looked even more uncomfortable. She mumbled something I didn't hear, and Palmer said: *'Hey, I made it worth your while, didn't I?'* Then he reached into his pocket and pulled out a wad of cash and waved it in her face... and he said: *'And there's more of this coming your way, if you keep your mouth shut.'*"

Aunt Olive finished and looked triumphantly at Ellie. "See? Isn't that proof?"

"Proof of what?"

"That Palmer is the murderer, dear! Or rather, he's behind the murder. He didn't actually do the deed himself—he paid someone else to do it and that 'someone' is Monica!"

Ellie gaped at her aunt.

"Think about it," Aunt Olive insisted. "It would

have been so easy for Monica to do it. After all, she was Brandi's therapist and she was in the room with the girl. We've all been looking in the wrong direction! We've been trying to guess who could have had the opportunity to sneak into the room, but we forgot to consider the person who was already *in* the room with Brandi. Monica could have pretended to be giving Brandi a treatment and then, when the girl was relaxed and defenseless, she could have used one of the cushions to smother her. Then she pretended to leave the room on some pretext, so that she could later claim that the murderer must have sneaked in while she was away."

"You can't know all this just from that conversation you overheard," protested Ellie. "Don't you think your imagination is running a bit wild and you're jumping to conclusions? I mean, you're basically suggesting that Palmer paid a spa therapist to bump Brandi off!" She gave an incredulous laugh.

"Why not? Palmer has a habit of paying people to silence them."

"There's a big difference between paying hush money and hiring someone to commit murder!"

Aunt Olive waved a dismissive hand. "Fiddle-faddle! There's no difference in the man's mind. He's used to using money to make problems go away. This is just another example of it. Come on, poppet! I saw him brandishing a wad of money at her!"

"Well, maybe... maybe he was talking about something else," said Ellie.

"Like what?" Aunt Olive demanded. "He called them 'partners in crime,' didn't he?"

"Yes, but that could just be a figure of speech. People use it all the time; it doesn't have to mean 'crime' literally," argued Ellie. "Besides, it doesn't make sense—why would Palmer want to kill one of his own bikini contestants?"

"That's easy. I've been talking to Sandy and she thinks Brandi may have been a threat to Palmer."

"Oh, yeah, she's told me that theory," said Ellie, frowning. "But it's just an idea of hers, isn't it? There's no actual report of Brandi—or any woman—accusing Palmer, is there?"

"Ahh... well, Sandy has been doing some digging around, and she heard via her contacts that there are rumors circulating about a big case being prepared against Don Palmer by an anonymous woman. And unlike previous cases, apparently this time there is proof, which could get him arrested for sexual assault."

"And they're saying this woman was Brandi?"

"Nobody knows who the woman was," Aunt Olive admitted. "They thought she was biding her time until she had prepared a solid enough case to go public with a big announcement. But the rumors did say that she was young and attractive."

Ellie snorted. "That could be half of Florida!"

Aunt Olive was undaunted. "I'm going to ring Detective Carson first thing in the morning! I'm sure this will crack the case wide open, as they say!"

***

The next morning, however, didn't bring the result that Aunt Olive hoped for. Carson diligently listened to her account of the overheard conversation, as well as her theories about Palmer's motive for murder, but he didn't seem impressed. And he certainly wasn't prepared to go after a well-known and powerful businessman on the basis of some wild accusations from a "hysterical" activist with a police record.

"It's just because Carson is biased against Sandy so he won't believe anything she says!" fumed Aunt Olive as she and Ellie walked back to their villa after a late lunch that afternoon. "He kept telling me that Palmer had an alibi for the time when the girls were out of their rooms last night, so he can't be the murderer."

Ellie was confused. "What do you mean? The murder was at the spa. What's last night got to do with that?"

"Well, Carson believes that the murderer and the person who left Roxy the threatening note are one and the same. So if Palmer couldn't have left the note, he couldn't be the murderer either, according to him. But that's rubbish!" said Aunt Olive angrily. "As I kept telling Carson, if Palmer could have paid Monica to kill Brandi, he could have paid someone else to break into Roxy's room and leave the doll and note."

"It seems a bit convoluted, though," said Ellie. "I mean, at this rate, Palmer seems to be paying everyone to commit a crime for him! And besides, if Sandy is saying that his original motive was to silence Brandi... well then, why is he now targeting the other girls?"

Aunt Olive didn't answer, although Ellie could see that her aunt's mind was furiously working as she tried to come up with a new line of argument. Then suddenly, Aunt Olive gripped her arm and yanked her sideways.

"Look!" Aunt Olive hissed, peering through the leaves of a large hibiscus bush next to them.

Ellie leaned forward and saw a man walking across the intersection of pathways up ahead. It was Don Palmer. He was dressed in a polo shirt and white tennis shorts, and carried a racket in one hand. As she watched, he turned toward the entrance to the courts as another man in tennis gear came out to greet him. Their voices drifted over:

"Hello, Mr. Palmer! Ready for your lesson?"

"Better go easy on me, Coach," growled Palmer. "I've got a hell of a hangover."

The men's voices faded as they walked out onto a tennis court. Aunt Olive stepped out from behind the hibiscus bush and turned to Ellie with a gleam in her eyes.

"This is our chance, poppet!"

"Chance for what?"

"For some snooping! Palmer will be tied up in his

tennis lesson for at least an hour, which means his room will be empty. Come on!"

"Wait—Aunt Olive—!"

Ellie found herself speaking to empty air. Her aunt was already hurrying away. For someone in her sixties, Aunt Olive could sure move fast! By the time she caught up with her aunt, Ellie was out of breath and sweating profusely. The day was incredibly warm, with the sun blazing down from a cloudless sky.

Ellie paused, puffing, next to her aunt and looked up at the building next to them. There was a sign attached to the wall which read: "Beachfront Suites Wing." A covered outdoor walkway ran past a row of doors, each no doubt leading into a suite. Aunt Olive had stopped in front of the last door and was bending over to examine the lock.

"You're not going to try to break in, are you?" said Ellie, aghast. "What if we're caught?"

"Who said anything about breaking in?" said Aunt Olive airily.

She straightened and looked down the walkway beyond Ellie. Then her expression brightened and she trotted off to the other end of the walkway. Ellie turned to see her aunt approaching a woman in a resort uniform who was standing beside a Housekeeping trolley. They talked for a few minutes, then her aunt returned, accompanied by the other woman.

"...so kind of you!" Aunt Olive was gushing. "It was

really so silly of me to lose my keys, but you know, one gets so forgetful in one's old age... and now I'm just desperate for the loo. I must have had too much orange juice at lunch and my bladder isn't what it used to be either... and it would take ages to walk back to the reception to get a new key..."

"Oh sure, ma'am... no problem," said the woman, pulling out her master card-key and bending towards Don Palmer's door.

A few minutes later, they were in. Aunt Olive thanked the maid profusely and waited until the latter had disappeared around the corner with her trolley before turning to Ellie and saying:

"Now, you go and have a good snoop around the whole suite, poppet."

"What?" said Ellie. "Why me?"

"Because I need to stay here and act as a lookout," said Aunt Olive briskly.

"But... what am I supposed to be looking for?" demanded Ellie.

"Anything that looks suspicious! Have a poke through his bags, rifle through any documents you find, check his toiletries for anything that looks unusual... Use your initiative, dear!"

"But—"

Before Ellie could argue further, she found herself propelled into the room and the door shut behind her. She paused just inside and heaved a sigh of exasperation. Then looked around the suite. Housekeeping had obviously already come and made up the room, and everything was clean and neat. She made a half-hearted attempt to search as her aunt had directed, but without having some idea of what to look for, it seemed like a completely random, pointless exercise.

Ellie was just heading back to the door when she froze. Outside, she could hear voices: Aunt Olive, sounding rather flustered, and a deep male voice.

Ellie's heart skipped a beat. She recognized the man's voice: it was Don Palmer!

CHAPTER EIGHTEEN

Ellie hovered just inside the front door, straining her ears to hear the voices outside and wondering frantically what to do.

"...can't talk, Mrs. Goldberg. Excuse me, but I've got a splitting headache and—"

"Oh, you poor dear! Headaches can be so nasty! Have you tried soaking your feet in hot water to draw blood from your head? Or yanking a handful of hair up very tight?"

"Huh?"

"They're old folk remedies for headaches that I found when I was doing research for a book—"

"Look, uh, Mrs. Goldberg—I don't mean to be rude but my head's killing me and I'd like to get back to my room."

"Oh... yes... of course... but—"

There was a beep as a card key was inserted into the door, then the handle began to turn.

Yikes! Ellie backed away from the door. *How am I going to explain to Don Palmer what I'm doing in his suite?*

Outside, she could hear her aunt making one more attempt to detain Palmer, and the businessman sounded quite irate now as he brushed her aunt off. Ellie looked around in a panic, then—as she spotted the pair of rubber gloves and checkered tea towel, draped over the side of the sink in the kitchenette area—she had an idea. It was a crazy, stupid idea, but she couldn't think of anything else.

She dived across the room and snatched up the tea towel, tying it quickly around her head like a headscarf. Then she opened the cabinet door beneath the sink and peered inside. There was the usual clutter of cleaning items and kitchenware. Ellie grabbed the small trashcan, which had just been emptied, and set it on the floor beside her, then began throwing in sponges, kitchen towels, scrubbing brushes, and any other cleaning equipment she could find under the sink. Finally, she draped the rubber gloves over the side, so that they could be prominently seen. Hopefully, from a distance, the plastic trashcan would resemble a cleaning caddy filled with items. Then she dived back into the under-sink cabinet.

By the time Don Palmer opened the door, she had half-crawled under the kitchen sink and all he could see was her bottom, peeking out from between the open cabinet doors and the "cleaning caddy" filled with equipment next to her. Ellie was thankful that she had chosen to wear chino shorts and a cotton blouse that morning. Her clothes might not have looked exactly like the resort's Housekeeping uniform, but she hoped they were good enough to fool Palmer from a distance. At least she wasn't wearing a sundress or some other outfit that made her look too obviously like a guest.

She heard the businessman stop short as he walked in and saw her. He made a sound of irritation and said:

"For Pete's sake, aren't you finished cleaning the room?"

Ellie put on the best American accent she could muster as she pretended to scrub industriously. "Sorry, sir... I'm almost done..."

Her pulse raced as she heard him come up behind her. She kept her head down and scrubbed even harder, hoping that the headscarf would help support her impromptu disguise. Although she had been briefly introduced to Don Palmer on the day they took the catamaran trip, she hadn't spent any time talking to him face-to-face, and Ellie hoped fervently that he wouldn't have any clear recollection of her.

"Hey... you don't look like the normal Housekeeping," said Palmer from behind her.

"Erm... I'm new... just started today and they

didn't have time to get me my uniform," mumbled Ellie.

It was a ludicrous explanation and she didn't have much hope that he'd believe her. She felt Palmer lean down, closer to her, and her heart pounded. If he made her turn around to face him, there was no way she could avoid being recognized. He came closer—she could hear his noisy breathing and smell the heavy aftershave he used—and Ellie had to fight the urge to flinch away.

"Oh, I hope they let you keep this outfit. I kinda like the way your ass looks in those shorts," said Palmer's breathy voice.

Then, to Ellie's shock and outrage, Palmer gave her bottom a hearty smack. She squealed in surprise and he laughed uproariously. Then he turned and headed into the bedroom. Ellie jerked out from under the sink and glared at his retreating back.

Oooh! The man was a total rat! She wanted to chase after Palmer and confront him for his outrageous behavior, or call resort security and report him for sexual harassment. But she restrained herself. Without any video footage as proof, it was only her word against his, and she was in an especially weak position, given that she was in the wrong for trespassing in his room and impersonating the resort staff. So Ellie took a deep breath and swallowed her anger, then she hurriedly shoved everything back under the sink, shut the cabinet, and practically ran for the door. She could hear

Palmer's shower starting as she let herself out of his suite.

"Great gibbons, Ellie—I was just beginning to get worried!" Aunt Olive exclaimed, hurrying up to her. Then she stopped and stared at Ellie's head. "What on earth are you wearing a tea towel on your head for?"

"Oh, this..." Ellie yanked it off and looked reproachfully at her aunt. "I was improvising, since you abandoned me in there to deal with Palmer alone."

"Well? Did you learn anything?" asked Aunt Olive eagerly.

"No... other than that Sandy O'Brien is right: Don Palmer is a giant sleazebag!" said Ellie. "The bastard made a disgustingly suggestive comment and smacked my bum. Ooh, how I'd love to report him!" She clenched her fists.

"You'll punish him more if you can get him for murder," said Aunt Olive with practical briskness. "So you didn't find anything at all?"

Ellie threw up her hands. "What is there to find? I had no idea what to look for!"

"Oh, for goodness' sake, poppet! I told you: anything that looks mysterious—"

"How do I know what 'mysterious' looks like?" asked Ellie in exasperation. "This isn't one of your books, Aunt Olive. There aren't convenient clues just lying around, waiting for the sleuth to find them."

Aunt Olive harrumphed and stalked away down

the path, with Ellie following. Somehow, they found themselves walking past the colonnade around the side of the main resort building, which housed a row of exclusive shops serving the resort guests. There was an art gallery, jeweler, designer boutique, a store selling delicious luxury chocolates, and a huge resort gift shop which sold all sorts of tourist souvenirs, vacation essentials, resort merchandise, beach clothing, and more. Aunt Olive's mood seemed to improve as they browsed the displays and she lingered outside the designer boutique window.

"Ooh! Now, isn't that gorgeous, poppet?" said Aunt Olive, eyeing a glamorous trouser suit in white silk. "I'm just going to pop in and see if they have it in my size!"

Ellie wandered down the rest of the row until she reached the resort's own gift shop, and was about to enter when she noticed a man loitering a short distance beyond the end of the colonnade. The path ended in a dead end there, with nothing more than an overgrown area of landscaping and greenery surrounding a small bench next to a tall palm tree. The man was standing by the bench, looking uneasily around.

Ellie stared at him thoughtfully. There was something odd in his manner, with the overtly casual way he had his hands shoved into his pockets and kept his head down, avoiding anyone's eyes... yet his very body language seemed to scream: *I'm skulking undercover!* But the main reason Ellie kept looking quizzically at him was because he looked awfully familiar. She was sure that she'd met him before, and yet she couldn't quite place him. Finally, after puzzling it over for several moments, she gave up.

He's probably just a guest that I've seen a few times around the resort, she reasoned as she wandered idly into the gift shop.

Almost as soon as she set foot inside, a middle-aged woman with a practiced smile and a predatory gleam in her eye slid out from behind the counter and hurried over.

"Well, hel-lo, honey!" she said, beaming at Ellie. "Haven't seen you in a long while!"

"Hi Lynne," said Ellie, giving the woman a wary smile in return.

Lynne, the gift shop manager, was warm and friendly—and an absolute fiend of a saleswoman. Ellie had already bought far too many things she didn't need, courtesy of Lynne's persuasive (and relentless!) technique. Now she looked hurriedly around for something to distract the woman, then she paused as her gaze alighted on a rack of newspapers beside the shop's entrance.

A bold headline grabbed her eye: "BREAKING NEWS: MURDERER STALKS BIKINI CONTEST AGAIN! WHO WILL BE NEXT?" Underneath the headline was an article describing the events of the night before in lurid detail, including a sensationalistic account of Roxy's "breakdown" and graphic descriptions of the damaged doll and threatening note.

Ellie frowned as she scanned the article. She could distinctly remember the police warning them all the night before not to speak to the press, as they didn't want details of the incident leaked, in case it hindered the investigation. Any information given to the public was to be controlled via official press conferences—the first of which wasn't planned until noon today.

But this paper came out this morning, thought Ellie. *So how has the media got hold of the information before the press conference has even taken place? And the amount of detail suggests an inside source, not just educated guesses by an imaginative reporter.*

Then she caught her breath as she saw the name on the byline—Ted Baxter—and she jerked her head back up to look out the shop doorway at the man loitering in the distance. *Of course! That's why he seemed so familiar!*

The man was Ted Baxter, a local reporter Ellie had met during her first week in Florida. He worked for the *Tampa Daily News* and had been covering the murder at the writers' conference, as well as Aunt Olive's "disappearance" at the time. In fact, he had hassled Ellie for an interview and peppered her with insinuations about her aunt. And it looked like he was up to his old tricks, sniffing out a story at the resort again.

"Is everything OK?"

Ellie jumped as she realized that Lynne had been

trying to get her attention for the last few minutes.

"Oh... sorry." She gave the woman an apologetic smile. "My mind wandered. Erm... that man there—" She pointed out the doorway. "—have you seen him around before?"

Lynne squinted into the distance. "Oh, him. Yeah, I've seen him hanging around a few times this week. Didn't think much of it. Why?"

"Oh... I just wondered what he was doing. He looks like he's waiting for something."

"More like some*one*," said Lynne, grinning. "The last couple of times, a young woman showed up to meet him."

"You mean a girlfriend?"

"Well, maybe not 'official,' if you know what I mean," said Lynne with a wink. "They were acting kinda furtive. You know, you get people here on vacation who sneak away from their other halves..."

"You mean they're having an affair?" said Ellie, disappointed that it was nothing more than a sordid cliché.

Lynne shrugged. "Hey, you see a lot of stuff going on in a resort—you learn not to judge, you know? But yeah, I wouldn't be surprised. She was real pretty. I think she might be someone connected to that bikini contest that's going on at the moment, actually. I think I've seen her around."

Ellie's ears pricked up. "Really? What did she look like?"

Lynne frowned. "Well, to be honest with you, I

didn't see her face exactly. She was wearing these big black shades and a wide-brimmed hat that covered most of her hair. But you could tell she was really pretty, you know? And she had a great figure. Well, you'd have to, wouldn't you, to enter a bikini contest?"

Ellie turned to look at the man in the distance again. Who was the young woman who had come to meet Ted Baxter? Was he really just here for a romantic tryst? Or was his skulking around related to the mystery of Brandi's murder and the ill-fated bikini contest?

CHAPTER NINETEEN

As Ellie continued watching, she saw Ted Baxter glance impatiently at his watch several times. Then he gave an irritated sigh, turned on his heel, and started down the path. He passed the gift shop without glancing inside and soon disappeared around the side of the colonnade.

"I guess he got tired of waiting for her to show up," said Lynne, chuckling. "Anyway, what can I help you with, honey?"

"Oh, nothing, really," said Ellie, dragging her attention back to the shop. "I... erm... I'm just browsing."

"Ah! Well, in that case, let me show you this new skincare range that's just arrived!

"Oh no, I—"

"These are awesome products, developed by a

local Tampa Bay company—yes, that's right!—and they're all eco-friendly and non-toxic. Here, try this..."

Ellie found herself dragged over to a shelf where Lynne grabbed a small glass tester bottle and pumped several squirts of lotion into her open palm. Then she smeared this liberally onto the back of Ellie's hand, saying:

"Feel that texture! Isn't it just wonderful? So fresh and dewy, and it absorbs instantly into the skin. And it's got the most wonderful fragrance too: 'Spring Jonquils.'" Lynne shoved the bottle against Ellie's nose.

Ugh! Ellie reeled back from the pungent scent emanating from the bottle. Her first instinct was to exclaim: "That's disgusting!" but somehow she heard herself saying instead: "Oh... yes... erm... that smells lovely."

Lynne beamed. "What did I tell ya? And we've got a special deal going on today: if you buy a bottle of this lotion, you'll get a tub of their Dream Cream for half price! Let me tell you, this cream is something else!" She unscrewed a small plastic tub and showed Ellie the pale green cream inside. "It's loaded with super ingredients, like grapeseed oil and green tea extract and pomegranate seed. Tea tree oil as well, to take care of any breakouts. Plus that lovely Spring Jonquils fragrance again."

Hastily, Ellie leaned back as Lynne waved the tub under her nose. "Thanks, but I really don't need—"

"Sure you do! You might think you're still young but it's never too early to start taking care of your skin! Now, how about a whitening serum?" continued Lynne relentlessly. "It'll do wonders for your freckles. I got my daughter some of this and now she *swears* by it! Speaking of family, how are your folks back in England?"

"Uh... they're fine—"

"Got any gifts for your mom yet?"

"No, but I'm not going back for a couple of weeks yet—"

"Hey, I bet she'd love a set of products from the Spring Jonquils range! Tell you what, I can do you a real nice gift basket with the lotion, anti-ageing serum, and nourishing cream... and I'll throw in a pot of eye gel as well. Whaddya say? I can wrap it up for you, make it super pretty... I've got beautiful gift paper right here... and I'll tie it all up with a bow, so it'll be all ready for you to just hand to your mom when you get home. I'm sure she'd love it. Skin care products all the way from Florida! And such an exclusive local brand..."

A few minutes later, Ellie staggered out of the gift shop carrying a bulging bag and an enormous gift-wrapped box, and bumped into Aunt Olive just coming to join her.

"Great gibbons, poppet! I leave you for fifteen minutes and you buy up half the gift shop," Aunt Olive teased.

"Just be grateful I didn't end up getting the

inflatable beach chair, the mermaid-themed lamps, and the giant Tampa Bay poster map as well," said Ellie darkly. She shook her head as she looked down at the packages in her hands. "I can't believe I just bought a whole range of creams and lotions with a stinky fragrance I can't stand."

"Why on earth did you buy them, then?" asked Aunt Olive, astonished. "Why didn't you just say you didn't like the smell?"

"It... it just felt too rude!" said Ellie helplessly. "Lynne was so enthusiastic and kept telling me to smell it and gushing about how wonderful the fragrance was—and I couldn't bring myself to say I thought it smelled disgusting." Ellie put a hand to her forehead and groaned. "I felt like I had to be polite and not hurt her feelings."

Aunt Olive chuckled. "That's the great British problem: the ridiculous compulsion to be polite all the time and not cause offense. The more awful it is, the more we feel compelled to say it's great! That's where we need to be more like the Americans, dear. They're much more straightforward and they aren't afraid to say what they think."

"Anyway, never mind the shopping—guess who I saw skulking around at the end of the colonnade?" Ellie said excitedly. She told her aunt about Ted Baxter and the newspaper article with his byline. "He's obviously been coming to meet someone here at the resort and Lynne says she saw an attractive young woman come to meet him. She thinks they're having an affair but I'll bet it's not that—I'll bet it's actually someone feeding him inside information about the contest and the murder investigation!"

"But what does all this have to do with Don Palmer?" asked Aunt Olive.

"Nothing," said Ellie impatiently. "I think you're barking up the wrong tree with Palmer—"

"I saw him! I heard him!" said Aunt Olive. "I'm telling you, he was up to something dodgy at the spa and Monica was involved. And he has the perfect motive! You've seen firsthand what a creep Palmer is and how he takes advantage of women. He wouldn't be the first man who is willing to do anything to silence women who could expose him and bring him to justice."

"Yes, but *murder*?" said Ellie. "I can understand him paying Brandi off, but to bribe someone else to kill her—isn't that just a bit too far-fetched?"

"No more far-fetched than you thinking that Gina murdered her to get more PR for the bikini contest," Aunt Olive retorted. "You're fixated on Gina because you're jealous of her."

"I'm not jealous of her!" cried Ellie, her voice shriller than she intended. She took a deep breath and made an effort to say in a calmer voice: "I admire Gina and the way she's so capable and confident—"

"But I'll bet a part of you secretly wishes that she turns out to be the murderer," said Aunt Olive with an impish smile.

"I do not! That's a ridiculous thing to say!"

spluttered Ellie angrily.

"Oh, it's perfectly understandable, poppet. If I were you, I would have wanted to claw her eyes out the minute she arrived and started eyeing Blake like he's an all-you-can-eat buffet," said Aunt Olive. "So you can't help being biased where Gina is concerned. It's only human nature, after all."

"I'm not biased!" Ellie insisted. "I honestly think she could be a suspect, simply based on the facts."

"We'll see," said Aunt Olive as she led the way back to their villa.

They dropped off Ellie's purchases, then decided to take a stroll on the beach to work off their big lunch.

"Do you mind if we pop around to Roxy's room first?" asked Ellie. "I'd like to see how she is after her scare last night."

"Oh, of course. Poor dear... That girl seemed to be having a difficult time at the contest already, and now this had to happen. I wonder, though, if maybe the threatening note hadn't been intended for her?" Aunt Olive mused as they began walking towards the outer wing where the contestants' rooms were located.

"What d'you mean?" asked Ellie, surprised. "Who else could it have been meant for?"

"Well... her roommate, perhaps."

"Amber?"

"Yes, think about it: I can't see Roxy being much of a threat to anyone, but Amber is a very different kettle of fish. Now *that* girl is someone who would never be afraid to speak up and cause offense. And her room was right next to Brandi's at the spa. Maybe she heard something or saw something which could incriminate Monica, and now Palmer is trying to intimidate her to keep her mouth shut!"

Ellie had to admit that it wasn't a bad theory, although she still had her doubts about the great Palmer-Monica conspiracy. Even if the businessman really had decided to resort to something as drastic as murder, surely someone as wealthy and powerful as Don Palmer would hire a professional hitman for the job and not rely on a random spa therapist?

Ellie was so deep in thought that she nearly tripped in surprise when a plaintive voice said: *"MIAOW!"* at her feet. She looked down to see a sleek black cat standing by her ankles and staring up at her with big green eyes.

"Hello, Mojito," said Ellie with a smile, bending to give the animal a pat. "I haven't seen you around for a while. What have you been getting up to?"

"MIAOW!" The cat sat up on her haunches and tucked her paws against her chest in the classic "beg" pose. She looked expectantly up at Ellie and gave another plaintive cry.

"Aww, bless..." said Aunt Olive, watching Mojito and smiling. "I think she wants you to pick her up for a cuddle!"

Ellie hesitated, then bent and scooped the cat up in her arms. Mojito settled comfortably against her

179

shoulder, purring loudly and looking around with interest from her higher vantage point.

"Why don't you bring her along to Roxy's room?" suggested Aunt Olive. "If the girl is feeling a bit down, a cuddle with the kitty ought to do her good."

"I'm not sure we should be taking Mojito into the guest rooms," said Ellie.

"Oh, fiddle-faddle! Do you think there's anywhere this cat hasn't got into?" Aunt Olive snorted.

Ellie grinned. "True."

Mojito did seem to have an uncanny knack of sneaking into every corner of the resort, even those— or perhaps *especially* those—where she was not supposed to be. Now, she gave a *chirrup* of delight as Ellie began walking again and she was carried along, enjoying a novel view of the resort grounds from human eye level.

They arrived at the wing where the bikini contestants' rooms were located and stopped outside the last door in the row. Aunt Olive knocked and, a minute later, the door swung open to reveal Roxy herself.

"Hi," she said, looking surprised.

"We just came to see how you're doing after last night's ordeal," said Ellie, adding with a grin as she held up the cat in her arms: "And we brought you some animal therapy."

Roxy's eyes lit up. "Aww, she's gorgeous! That's Mojito, the resort cat, right? I've seen her around but haven't gotten to pat her yet."

"Here," said Ellie, leaning over.

Roxy reached out and took Mojito in her arms, cuddling her close. The cat wrinkled her nose and sneezed, then squirmed suddenly, fighting to get free. Roxy struggled to hold on for a moment, then gave up, dropping the cat to the ground. Mojito landed nimbly on all fours and shook herself before trotting away without a backward glance.

"What on earth got into her?" asked Ellie, staring after the retreating feline.

"Are you wearing a strong perfume? Some cats hate that," said Aunt Olive, sniffing the air.

"No. I've only got some sunscreen on," said Roxy.

"Bronzed Babe?" asked Ellie quickly and, at Roxy's nod, she said, "That must be it! I was using some by the pool yesterday and Mojito hissed at me too. It really reeks of pineapples."

"If it smells that strong to you, it must be overpowering for a cat. Animals have much more sensitive noses," said Aunt Olive.

"It *is* a little strong," Roxy agreed with a laugh. She beckoned them into the room. "Anyway, come on in."

"Where's Amber?" Ellie asked, looking around the empty room as she and Aunt Olive followed the other girl into the suite.

"She's with Gina and the other girls. They've all gone over for a practice rehearsal on the raised catwalk that the resort has erected on the south lawn, but I didn't really feel like joining in. I mean, what's the point? The contest is likely to be canceled anyway," said Roxy with a sigh.

Ellie raised her eyebrows. "Really? I thought it was just 'on hold' until they sort out the investigation—"

"Yes, but that's going nowhere!" said Roxy. "The police don't have any real suspects—Gina told us this morning. At first, they thought it was that protestor woman, but now they don't think it's her and they've got no other strong leads. So it could drag on forever."

"What about the note from last night?" asked Ellie.

Roxy shrugged. "Gina says they can't tell if it's the same person who committed the murder. She keeps saying it's just some stupid prank—that's why she's pushing for the contest to go ahead—but Mr. Palmer is really pissed about the whole thing. He started talking about canceling the contest altogether, 'cos everything is so messed up now. He was like: 'I don't want my brand associated with murder.'" She sighed again. "You know, I'm kinda over the whole thing. Part of me just wants to go home now."

"Where do you live?" asked Ellie.

Roxy gave her a small smile. "Oh, this small town in the middle of nowhere. You wouldn't have heard of it. It's got, like, a few shops on the main street, a diner, a church, and a high school, and that's it. There aren't even any—"

Aunt Olive, who had been silent for a while now, suddenly burst out: "High school!"

The two girls gaped at her.

"The victim's background!" said Aunt Olive excitedly. "That's what we haven't considered so far. We've been so busy looking at everyone who could be a suspect, but what we should have been doing is looking at the victim herself. If I was plotting one of my books, that's where I would start: map out the victim's background and decide whether she'd done something that might come back to haunt her." She wagged a finger in their faces. "I'll bet the answer to Brandi's murder is in her past!"

Whirling, she rushed out the door and they could hear her voice fading as she hurried away: *"... must try to contact her high school... maybe get hold of the yearbook... and any past employers... wonder if Monica might come from the same town? And what about ex-boyfriends..."*

Roxy turned back to Ellie. "Wow—is she always like that?"

Ellie laughed. "Yeah, she goes off like that whenever she gets an idea for a plot or a character. And if her books are anything to go by, Aunt Olive won't rest now until she's dug up every last thing she can find about Brandi's past."

"Wouldn't the police have already done that?" asked Roxy.

"I suppose so. But I bet they won't be as thorough as Aunt Olive! They're busy and under pressure from a lot of cases, whereas she'll treat it like a personal obsession. I mean, this is what she does for a living, you know: research things for her novels. She loves the challenge."

Roxy sighed wistfully. "You've got such a cool aunt. Mine just tells me I should lose some weight."

"You? Lose weight?" said Ellie, looking at the other girl's svelte figure in astonishment.

Roxy blushed. "Well, I used to be a lot fatter. Like, you know, really big. You wouldn't recognize me if you saw my high school photo."

"Well, you've done a fantastic job," said Ellie admiringly. "Next time I need dieting tips, I'm going to come to you!"

Roxy looked at her shyly. "You don't need any dieting tips. You've got a great figure too."

"I'd hardly qualify for a bikini contest. But thank you," said Ellie, smiling at the other girl warmly. "Well, I'd better get going. I just wanted to check that you're OK. I'm glad you seem to have recovered from your scare."

"Thanks, that's super sweet of you. You've really cheered me up, you know. I think I might go and join the other girls, after all," said Roxy brightly.

She collected a few items, then followed Ellie out of the room, making sure that the door was locked behind her. The two girls walked together to the large lawn overlooking the beach. The raised stage with a catwalk protruding in a T-shape stood in the center of the lawn, but it was empty and, when they asked one of the resort staff assembling some equipment, they were told that the group of contestants had moved on.

"I wonder where they went?" said Roxy, looking anxious now that she might've been missing out on the activities.

"Hiya, Roxy!"

They turned to see Nikki coming out onto the terrace of a ground-floor suite nearby. She slid the French door carelessly shut behind her and hurried over to join them.

"You missed the rehearsal on the catwalk!" she said to Roxy.

Roxy hung her head. "Yeah, sorry. I was, like, feeling kinda down."

"Don't worry—Gina says we're gonna have another rehearsal tomorrow morning."

"Where's everyone now?" asked Roxy.

Nikki pointed down a path which curved around the lawn and led out onto the beach. "They're all down in that area with the palm trees and dunes and hammocks. That photographer dude is here again and we're gonna do some pics on the hammocks." She jerked a thumb at the French doors behind her. "I was just dropping some stuff off for Gina in her room, then I'm going back to join them."

"OK, cool. I'll come with you," said Roxy eagerly.

"I won't join you, but have fun," said Ellie, waving them off.

She turned to retrace her steps, then paused as something caught her eye. The French door of Gina's suite was not fully closed—Nikki obviously hadn't slid it properly shut in her haste—and there was a narrow gap showing between the glass door and the frame. Ellie stared at it and an insidious little thought suddenly formed in her mind: *If Aunt Olive thinks we can snoop in Don Palmer's room, then why can't I snoop in Gina's room?*

After all, Gina was just as much of a suspect as Palmer, she reasoned. Then an echo of Aunt Olive's voice sounded in her head: *"You're just fixated on Gina because you're jealous of her."*

No, that's not true! thought Ellie hotly. *I'm not biased. There really is something that doesn't add up with Gina and I'm going to get to the bottom of it. If she's really innocent, then it won't matter—but if she's not, then at least I'll be able to prove to Blake and Aunt Olive that I wasn't just accusing her out of petty jealousy!*

Her mind made up, Ellie glanced quickly around to make sure that no one was watching her, then she walked casually over to Gina's terrace. Trying to act like she was just returning to her own room, Ellie crossed the terrace and slid the French door fully open, then—with a last furtive glance over her shoulder—she stepped inside.

CHAPTER TWENTY

It was cool and dark in the suite, and Ellie had to pause a moment to let her eyes adjust after the brightness outside. Then she began moving briskly around, making a systematic search of the place. It was surprisingly untidy; somehow, Ellie had expected Gina to have a super neat room, with everything organized and arranged efficiently. Instead, she found clothes strewn on the bed, papers and folders piled high on the dining table, and cartons of paraphernalia associated with the contest stacked in various corners.

One thing immediately caught her eye: a large, wide-brimmed straw hat thrown across the back of the couch. She suddenly remembered what Lynne at the gift shop had said about Ted Baxter meeting a young, attractive woman with "a wide-brimmed hat that covered most of her hair." If Gina was the woman meeting Ted Baxter, then she could've been the leak to the press. It would certainly tie in with her covert plan to generate publicity for the contest. If that was the case... Ellie looked around the room with new interest. Maybe she could find a paper trail of some sort, showing Gina's secret contact with the media—for example, correspondences with Ted Baxter.

Of course, most stuff is probably done online or at least on a password-protected computer these days, Ellie conceded. *Still, it doesn't hurt to look, does it?*

She poked around in the cartons and rifled through some of the folders, but although she found a few copies of the *Tampa Daily News* and a stack of Sandy O'Brien's homemade flyers, there was nothing that looked overtly suspicious. She was just about to start searching through several large canvas totes filled with Bronzed Babe products and other beach supplies when she heard a familiar squawking sound.

Uh-oh, thought Ellie.

Sure enough, when she turned around, she saw an enormous scarlet macaw land on the terrace outside in a flurry of red, blue, and brilliant green feathers.

"PEEKABOO!" croaked Hemingway, cocking his head and eyeing her through the open French door.

Ellie lunged for the glass door, but she was too slow. Before she could reach it, Hemingway had taken off again and swooped through the opening into the room. With a loud flap of his wings, he landed on top of Gina's TV.

"Arrghh!" said Ellie, cursing herself for not shutting the French door after she'd stepped inside.

Hemingway must have been perched up in one of the trees around the pool, as he often liked to do, and been watching her the whole time she had been with Roxy and Nikki. When he saw her sneak into Gina's suite, it must have piqued his curiosity and he had decided to come and join the fun.

Ellie looked at the parrot in exasperation. "Why must you always follow me everywhere?" She took a deep breath and let it out. "OK... just please be a good boy and be *quiet*," she pleaded.

The parrot responded by giving an ear-splitting screech.

"*Shush!*" Ellie hissed, glaring at him.

Hemingway ignored her and flew across to land on the couch. He peered at the canvas totes which she had been about to inspect and reached out with his beak to nibble one of the handles.

"Hey! Leave that alone," said Ellie, reaching out and hastily moving the bag out of his reach.

The parrot turned to Gina's wide-brimmed hat lying on the couch and grabbed it with his beak. Making a happy chattering sound, he began ripping the straw fibers out and shredding them.

"*Hemingway!* Stop that!" Ellie snatched the hat away from him, feeling like she was dealing with a demented three-year-old with wings.

Undaunted by her rebuke, the parrot waddled across to a canvas tote that had been tossed onto the other side of the couch and poked his head into the bag. He fished something out: it was a large vinyl pouch, with the zipper partially undone. Hemingway flung his head from side to side and made excited hooting noises at the sound of rattling coming from inside the pouch. A couple of items fell out: a lip gloss, an eyeliner pencil, and a tube of mascara. The pouch must have been a make-up bag, probably with things for last-minute touch-ups for the girls during the photoshoots.

Ellie gasped as she heard a loud splintering sound. Hemingway had picked up the eyeliner pencil in one of his claws and was holding it like a lollipop while crunching the end with his powerful beak. The pencil snapped suddenly in two and fragments of wood and kohl fell around him.

"Hemingway!" Ellie cried in dismay. "Stop it! You're breaking it!"

"*FRANKLY, MY DEAR, I DON'T GIVE A DAMN,*" the parrot squawked.

Ellie tried to snatch the make-up pouch from him. Her heart sank at the thought of Gina returning and finding all this damage and mess. There was no way the blonde woman wouldn't realize that someone had been trespassing in her room!

Hemingway gave an indignant screech as Ellie caught hold of the pouch and pulled it out of his beak. He stretched his neck out and snatched it back. Then he took off, carrying the pouch with him as he flew across the room to the kitchenette. It must have been heavier and more unwieldy than he expected, though, because it slipped from his grip and fell, bouncing off the kitchen counter and disappearing behind it. Ellie winced as she heard it smacking onto the floor.

"Great," she muttered, hurrying around the counter and surveying the mess in dismay.

Half the contents of the pouch had spilled out when it hit the floor, leaving a scattered pile of broken lipsticks, cracked powder compacts, shattered foundation bottles, and loose powder everywhere. Ellie groaned and crouched down to pick everything up. She was just wondering how best to wipe the smears of color from the floor tiles when she heard something that made her freeze.

It was Blake's voice and it sounded disturbingly close, as if he were on the terrace right outside the French doors. The next moment, she gulped as she heard Gina's honeyed tones as well, drifting in through the open glass doorway.

"...should be on the coffee table in my room, honey. Do you want me to come and look?"

"No, it's fine—I'll get it," said Blake.

Ellie raised herself slightly and peeked over the top of the kitchen counter. She saw Blake coming towards the French doors, then pausing and frowning.

"Did you know that the door on your terrace is open?" he called back over his shoulder.

"Really? I guess Nikki must have forgotten to shut it," came Gina's voice. "I sent her back to drop some things off for me. Maybe she left the room via the terrace door and didn't shut it all the way afterward."

"Well, you'd better tell her to be more careful. It's a security risk—anyone could have gotten in. With all the stuff happening at the moment, you don't want to invite more trouble," said Blake as he stepped through the open glass door and came into the suite.

Ellie jerked quickly back down behind the counter and silently prayed that Blake would not come over to the kitchenette. She could hear him moving around on the other side of the room. The next minute, she heard him exclaim in surprise.

"What the—!"

Footsteps came closer. Ellie tensed, bracing herself to be discovered any moment. Then the air was split by raucous squawking.

"*HOUSTON, WE HAVE A PROBLEM!*" screeched Hemingway.

Ellie groaned silently. She'd forgotten all about Hemingway! From the sound of it, the parrot was perched on one of the bar stools beside the kitchen.

"Hey buddy... how did you get in here?" Blake said from the other side of the counter.

"Blake?" Gina's voice drifted in from outside. "Honey, what's that racket?"

"It's OK," called Blake, rounding the side of the counter. "It's just the—"

He stopped short as he saw Ellie crouched low behind the counter. Their eyes met and Ellie held her breath. Would Blake give her away? She saw Blake's eyes flicker as he took in the open make-up pouch with all the spilled items. It was obvious that she had broken in and been snooping in Gina's room.

"Blake? What's going on?" came Gina's voice again from outside.

"Uh…" Blake hesitated as Ellie looked pleadingly at him. Then he raised his voice and called: "Nothing. It's just the parrot… Hemingway… He got into your room somehow and made a bit of a mess."

"*What?*"

There was the sound of rapid footsteps approaching, then Gina's voice sounding much louder and closer as she said: "What did he do?"

"Nothing… nothing… it's no big deal," said Blake quickly.

"*LIAR!*" squawked Hemingway. "*PANTS ON!*"

Blake held out his forearm to the parrot who—to Ellie's relief—immediately hopped on. Then the two of them walked back across to the French doors. They met Gina just as she was about to step in.

"What do you mean—oh!" Gina sounded a bit taken aback to be confronted suddenly by the enormous scarlet macaw.

Hemingway let out a loud screech and spread his wings, flapping them energetically. "*NASTY*

BROCCOLI! NASTY BROCCOLI!"

"Come on, let's just get him out of here," said Blake, blocking Gina's way into the room.

She backed out and Blake stepped outside after her, with the parrot still perched on his forearm. Ellie heard the French door slide shut after him and she breathed a huge sigh of relief. Carefully, she raised herself to peek over the edge of the counter. She could see Blake leading Gina away, with Hemingway now balancing on his shoulder, nibbling on his sun-streaked hair. She smiled at the sight, then felt a rush of gratitude toward Blake. He could have given her away, but instead he had decided to distract Gina and help her—even though he wasn't happy with her suspecting his ex-girlfriend. Ellie felt something warm fill her heart.

But there was no time to dwell on it now. She had to clean up this mess and get out of the suite before Gina returned. Hastily, she began scooping up the spilled items and stuffing them back into the make-up bag. One lipstick had lost its cap and rolled half under the mini-fridge. Ellie heaved a sigh of annoyance as she flattened herself to the floor to reach under the fridge and retrieve it. As she sat back up with the lipstick in her hand, she was overwhelmed by a strong artificial smell of raspberries.

"Eeuw..." Ellie wrinkled her nose. She was just about to put the cap back on the lipstick when she stopped. Slowly, she twisted the tube so that more of the lipstick was exposed and held it up to her nose for a careful sniff.

Yes! It was the same strong raspberry scent which had come off the threatening note left with the damaged Barbie doll! Ellie swiped the lipstick across the back of her hand and stared down at the glittery pink color. It matched the writing on the note as well.

What did this mean? Was Gina the one who had written that threatening note? Was that why she kept downplaying it as "a stupid prank"? Ellie suddenly remembered the other woman's words in Roxy's room last night: "...*look at this! It's written using lipstick or something, like one of those scented glitter lipsticks...*"

Could Gina really tell just by looking at the note that it had been written in lipstick? Or had she said that because she had *known* what was used to write it? Ellie remembered the way Gina had carelessly handled the note, leaving her own prints on it and contaminating the evidence. Was that a genuine mistake or a deliberate attempt to make sure that if her prints were found on the note, she would have a ready explanation?

Ellie's mind was churning as she let herself out of Gina's suite and walked slowly back to her own villa. If Gina was the one responsible for the threatening note, was she also responsible for the other attempts at sabotage? Ellie reflected that since the "incidents" had begun, the bikini contest had been continually in the news. And during the press briefings, Gina had always expertly answered questions in such a way as to put a positive spin on Don Palmer's company. She talked up their heritage and made sure to emphasize that past winners of the contest had gone on to successful careers. It was a masterful campaign at using the media to convert bad publicity into an advantage.

Watching her during those press conferences, Ellie had admired Gina's ability to quickly capitalize on something that had happened. But what if it hadn't been random—what if Gina had actually engineered it to happen?

Still, there was a big difference between setting up some fake incidents to grab media attention and killing one of the contestants. How far was Gina willing to go? Sabotage was one thing... but would she go as far as murder?

CHAPTER TWENTY-ONE

When Ellie returned to the villa, she expected to find Aunt Olive busily doing online research or pumping someone on the phone for information, but the place was empty.

"Aunt Olive?" Ellie called as she stepped in and shut the door.

There was no answer, and a quick search of the villa showed that her aunt wasn't there. Ellie frowned as she returned to the living room. Where had Aunt Olive gone? Her laptop was open on the dining table, and there was a half-drunk cup of tea, as well as a messy stack of scribbled notes, next to the computer. Ellie leaned over to look at the notes and saw Brandi's name amongst the scribblings. It looked like Aunt Olive had been busily researching Brandi's background and then decided to pop out in the middle of her work.

Maybe she's taking a break and gone out for a walk and a bit of fresh air, thought Ellie.

The silence was suddenly broken by a distinct beeping tune. Ellie recognized it as her aunt's ringtone. She was surprised that it seemed to be coming from beneath the pile of papers next to the laptop. Scrabbling through them, she finally unearthed an iPhone in an expensive-looking rose-gold case. Yes, definitely Aunt Olive's phone, but why was it here?

She must have forgotten to take it with her when she went out, thought Ellie. It wouldn't be the first time her aunt had left her phone behind—like many a scatterbrained author, Aunt Olive was notorious for misplacing things or leaving them in random places. Ellie remembered the time she had spent two hours searching the area around the pool after dinner because her aunt couldn't find her phone and couldn't remember where she might have left it. As it turned out, it had been buried, forgotten, at the bottom of the beach tote she had been using the day before.

Now, Ellie looked uncertainly at the ringing device. She was tempted to let the answering service take over, but the insistent ringing finally goaded her into answering the call.

"Hello?"

"Oh, is that Mrs. Goldberg? Ruth Blaise here, from the Riverfell High School Library," came a gushing voice. "First of all, can I just say again, ma'am, how exciting it was to get your call earlier... Oh my goodness, you're my very favorite author! To actually be talking to you in person... I can't tell you how much it has made my day! I had to pinch myself several times, you know, during our phone call... and having you ask me for help with your research was just the icing on the cake. I feel like a regular sleuth now—haha! The next time I read one of your books, I'll feel like I'm personally involved! Not that this is for your novels, of course, but still, you never know... they do say life inspires art, don't they?"

The woman paused at last for a breath and Ellie hurriedly said:

"I'm sorry—I'm not actually Olive Goldberg. I'm her niece. But I can take a message for her, if you like?"

"Ohhh! Silly me!" Ruth gave a nervous giggle. "Well, I guess I could always call back later—in fact, I was originally thinking I'd leave it until tomorrow morning, but then I remembered how urgent your aunt said it was and how the police are relying on her."

"Relying on her?" said Ellie in surprise.

"Oh, didn't you know? Mrs. Goldberg told me that the police had enlisted her to help with the murder investigation, since her experience as a mystery writer enabled her to provide a unique perspective."

"*What?*" Ellie shook her head in disbelief at Aunt Olive's blatant lies. Then, hastily recovering, she added, "Erm... that's right... but you can give me the information and I'll pass it straight on to Aunt Olive. I'm... uh... her research assistant."

"Ah, right. Well, after my chat with your aunt earlier, I got to thinking and I realized that there was something I'd forgotten to mention. Your aunt asked me if there was anything I remembered about Brandi Harris—any scandal she was involved in at school— and I'd told your aunt about a few small things. But I'd completely forgotten about something that happened in her senior year, right after Prom Night. Well, actually, it really started on the night of the prom. Brandi was the leader of a gang of girls—I guess you could say they were the 'popular' crowd— and they decided to play a nasty prank on one of the other girls: they gave her some facial cream which they claimed was a miracle cure for acne. But in fact, they'd tampered with it and mixed in a high dosage of glycolic acid. You know, that's the stuff they use in chemical peels for the face. A controlled amount is fine, but an overdose can burn your skin. Well, that's what happened to this poor girl. She used the cream the night before the prom and ended up with chemical burns and raw, peeling skin all over her face."

"Oh my God," said Ellie. "Was she all right?"

"She didn't need to be hospitalized, but they said she might end up with permanent scarring. The incident was brought before the principal, but since it was the end of the year and Brandi was leaving already, they decided not to make a big deal out of it."

"So she was never punished?"

"Not really."

"And the girl—the one they played the prank on—do you remember her name?" asked Ellie urgently.

"Hmm... I think it started with an A... something like Amy or Abby or Anna... maybe Amanda..."

"Amber?" suggested Ellie. "Could it have been Amber?"

"It could have been. I'm sorry—" Ruth gave a sheepish laugh. "—it was almost ten years ago and my memory isn't what it used to be."

"Would there have been a report about this in the local press anywhere?"

"Possibly, although I do remember that Brandi's parents wanted to hush things up as quickly as possible. And I think the victim was so upset and embarrassed that she didn't want her face in the papers."

"What about Brandi's parents—do they still live in the area?" asked Ellie. "Would it be easy to get in touch with them?"

"Oh, no, I believe they were killed in a car accident a couple of years after Brandi graduated."

"Oh, right," said Ellie, disappointed. She realized that she should have suspected that, given the lack of family that had shown up since Brandi's murder. "Well, thanks so much for calling back. I'll make sure my aunt gets the information; I'm sure it'll be a great help—"

"Oh, and do tell Mrs. Goldberg that if she's ever in this neck of the woods, she should drop by the school library! We have several of her books and I'd love for her to sign a couple of copies!"

***

Ellie stared thoughtfully into space for several moments after she'd hung up. The conversation with Ruth Blaise had set her mind buzzing over the mystery again and she mulled over the new information. Could Aunt Olive have been on the right track? Could a cruel high-school prank from seven years ago have been the real reason for Brandi's murder? In that case, who was the girl—the "victim"—who had suffered at Brandi's hands, and who would now want revenge?

Amber was the obvious choice but Ellie was reluctant to give up her suspicions about Gina. After all, "Gina" *could* sound a bit like "Anna," couldn't it? And what about Monica, the spa therapist? She was of a similar age, and there would be some kind of poetic justice in her killing her teenage nemesis in a spa while having a facial. It was a bit of a stretch, though, to imagine that "Monica" could sound enough like "Anna" for Ruth Blaise to confuse the names.

A loud knock on the villa door interrupted her thoughts. Ellie felt a twinge of dismay when she opened it to find Blake standing on the threshold, his handsome face creased in a frown.

"What were you doing in Gina's room?" he asked without preamble as he came in.

Ellie gulped and, for one moment, considered making up some excuse. Then she stopped herself. Blake deserved the truth, especially after he'd made the effort to help her earlier.

"I was snooping around," she admitted with a rueful look. "I'm sorry, I know you don't agree with me, but I still think Gina could be involved in Brandi's murder. There are just too many odd coincidences, like... did you know that she had a stash of Benadryl? I found a packet amongst Amber's toiletries and she told me they were from Gina, who keeps a supply for emergencies—"

"Anyone can buy Benadryl from the drugstore," said Blake impatiently.

"—and Gina was probably meeting a reporter from the *Tampa Daily News* in secret and leaking information about the investigation. That would tie in with her wanting to generate publicity for the contest and keep it in the headlines." Ellie hurried on as Blake looked like he was going to interrupt again. "And aside from all this, there's her false alibi on the day of the murder, when she lied about where she was in the spa—"

"I've asked her about that," Blake cut in. "And Gina admitted to me that she lied to the police."

CHAPTER TWENTY-TWO

Ellie stared disbelievingly at Blake. "Gina admitted that she lied?"

"Yes, she didn't go to the restroom, like she claimed. But she didn't go to Brandi's room to murder her either," said Blake, giving Ellie a dry look. "What she really did was go to the changing room and stuff some feminist propaganda flyers into the girls' bags."

"Gina was the one who did that? Not Sandy O'Brien?" said Ellie. "Oh! I remember now: I saw a stack of those flyers in Gina's room and I wondered why she had them." She shook her head. "So Sandy *was* telling the truth. She never went to the spa that day and she *was* being used as a scapegoat."

"Yeah," said Blake with a look of chagrin.

"But... why?" asked Ellie. "Why would Gina want

to distribute those flyers? Is she secretly part of some feminist movement?"

"No, it was just a ploy to get more publicity," admitted Blake. "Gina saw an opportunity to create more controversy around the contest. She told me that when Sandy O'Brien accosted you guys in the lobby the day before, it gave her the idea and she decided to 'help' Sandy's campaign along, knowing full well that it would generate more news and media attention."

"So I was right about her motives," said Ellie.

"Yes, but only for this—not for Brandi's murder," said Blake quickly. "Gina's not involved in that; she never expected something like that to happen! I mean, she wanted to get publicity for the contest, but not get it stalled or canceled by a homicide investigation! Think about it: how is that going to help her put on a successful event?"

Ellie was silent. Blake had a point. Still, she wasn't willing to give up so easily. "Why didn't Gina tell the police the truth, then, when she was questioned? After all, her actions ended up incriminating Sandy by making the police think that Sandy had sneaked into the spa. Gina nearly let an innocent woman get arrested for murder."

Blake looked uncomfortable. "She said she didn't think it would ever get to that—she was sure the police would release Sandy after questioning her. And if they hadn't, then she *would* have come forward and told them the truth."

But in the meantime, she didn't want anyone to know what a conniving cow she had been, thought Ellie dourly.

"And what about the other incidents of sabotage?" she asked. "Was that Gina's work too? To provide more fodder for the media?"

"No, she says none of that was her doing. She swore to me that the only thing she did was distribute those flyers in the spa that day. OK, I know that was dishonest, but in the grand scheme of things, it's hardly a huge crime, right?"

"What about the threatening note that Roxy found?" asked Ellie.

"Gina said she had nothing to do with that."

"In that case, how come she has a lipstick that's identical to the one used to write that note?" asked Ellie.

Blake frowned. "What are you talking about?"

Ellie described the lipstick she had found in the make-up pouch in Gina's room.

"But anyone could have had access to that pouch," protested Blake. "It's not Gina's personal make-up bag, right? You said the pouch was in a beach tote containing props and equipment for the contest, which means it was probably sitting around during photoshoots and anyone could have slipped something in there. So maybe someone put the lipstick in there to hide it or to incriminate Gina... or maybe the lipstick was originally in there and whoever wrote the note just 'borrowed' it to use, then put it back."

Ellie looked at Blake in frustration. Why did he always have to have a ready excuse to defend his ex-girlfriend? "You just don't want to believe that Gina could be guilty of anything," she muttered.

"That's not true," said Blake quickly. "I think she behaved really badly at the spa. But she swore to me that she's not responsible for this and I trust her..." He paused, then added, looking Ellie straight in the eye: "The same way I trusted you when I found that you'd sneaked into her room and were searching the place without permission. I trust your good intentions, even if I may not agree with your actions."

Ellie bit her lip. Then she took a deep breath and let it out slowly. OK, so maybe she was a bit biased where Gina was concerned, and maybe she had to let go of her conviction that Blake's ex was the murderer...

"Do you honestly feel that Gina is the only person who seems guilty?" asked Blake.

"No," Ellie admitted. "There are others too. In fact, I've just had a new lead." Quickly, she told Blake about her conversation with the librarian at Riverfell High School. "If Aunt Olive is right and the answer to the mystery lies in Brandi's past, then this girl—the one she played the prank on—could be someone with a lot of pent-up resentment and anger, who would have a very good motive for wanting to kill Brandi." She hesitated, then cleared her throat and said: "Erm... I don't suppose you know which high school

Gina went to?"

"I do, and it wasn't called Riverfell High," said Blake.

"Oh. Well... erm... that leaves all the other girls in the contest, although Amber is the most likely suspect. And there's also Monica."

"Monica?"

"She's the therapist at the spa who did Brandi's treatment," said Ellie.

"Ah... we call them 'technicians' in America."

"Really?" said Ellie, momentarily distracted. She wrinkled her nose. "That sounds like someone who fixes machinery or computers."

"Well, therapist sounds like someone who's going to psychoanalyze you and give you counseling," Blake retorted with a grin.

Ellie laughed. It was good to diffuse the tension at last and restore the usual warm camaraderie between them.

"You say 'potato,' I say 'po-tah-to,'" she joked.

"More like you say 'chips,' I say 'French fries,'" said Blake, chuckling. "But at least we're talking normally to each other again."

Ellie smiled. "OK, so—where was I? Oh yeah, Aunt Olive saw Monica coming out of Don Palmer's room last night and she overheard them say some things which sounded suspicious—"

"Like what?"

"Like Palmer calling them 'partners in crime' and warning Monica not to tell anyone 'what happened at the spa.'" She sighed. "I told Aunt Olive those could have innocent explanations, but she's convinced that there's a conspiracy between Palmer and Monica. She thinks that he paid the therapist—I mean the technician—to bump Brandi off. I thought it was a completely ludicrous idea at first! I mean, technically, it could have been done—in fact, Monica was probably the best-placed person to kill Brandi— but in practice, I just couldn't believe that she would have risked her job, her freedom, her life as she knew it, for a client who offered her a bit of extra money on the side. It's not as if she's a professional hitman or something!" Ellie held up a finger. "*But* it would be different if there was a *personal* element to it. If Monica was the girl at Riverfell High—if she had a *personal* grudge against Brandi—then she might have had extra incentive to agree to do it."

"Don't you think it's too much of a coincidence that the one technician that Don Palmer approaches also happens to be the one girl who had been bullied by Brandi?" said Blake skeptically.

Ellie gave a sheepish laugh. "Yeah, I suppose... But then who does that leave us?"

"There's Amber. I know you keep saying that she's the obvious suspect, but just because something is the obvious answer doesn't have to mean it's the *wrong* answer."

"True," said Ellie. "Maybe I need to speak to Amber again and confront her directly. OK, I'm going to look for her now—"

"Better get in line," said Blake dryly.

"What d'you mean?"

"She hasn't been seen all afternoon and the other girls have no idea where she's gone. Apparently, it's not the first time she's disappeared without explanation. She's never been much of a team player and Gina was just complaining to me that Amber's done this a few times before. She's getting pretty fed up with it."

Ellie stared at Blake, an uneasy feeling suddenly washing over her. She glanced at the dining table, with the open laptop and the scribbled notes scattered across the surface, and she wondered again where Aunt Olive had disappeared to.

"What?" asked Blake, picking up on her unease.

"Nothing. I just..." Ellie hesitated, then she turned an anxious face to Blake. "I can't explain it but I'm worried about Aunt Olive. I thought she'd be here, researching Brandi's background, but she seems to have suddenly gone off somewhere, and now you're telling me that Amber has suddenly disappeared too..." She trailed off uncertainly.

"Your aunt is probably somewhere on the resort grounds," said Blake reassuringly. He took Ellie's arm gently. "Come on, I'll help you look for her. Don't worry, I'm sure we'll find her."

CHAPTER TWENTY-THREE

They split up to search. With his longer legs and ability to cover more ground, Blake offered to take the beach and the outer areas of the resort whilst Ellie searched the buildings and pool area. She jogged around the familiar walkways, checked the tennis courts, scanned the tables in the various eateries and restaurants, but there was no sign of a spry lady in her sixties with curly grey hair and a glamorous fashion sense.

The sun had set now and twilight was falling, so guests were beginning to gather around the Tiki Bar by the pool for the resort's famous "Happy Hour." Aunt Olive was a big fan of the evening cocktail tradition and Ellie hoped that her aunt might be there, flirting with Paolo, the handsome bartender behind the counter. There was no sign of her, though, on any of the stools by the bar.

"Paolo, have you seen my aunt, by any chance?" Ellie asked.

The bartender looked up from the cocktail he was stirring and shrugged his shoulders. "No, sorry, ma'am."

Ellie sighed and turned away to continue searching. At last, she found herself on the first floor of the main resort building. She did a quick survey of the lobby, hoping to spot Aunt Olive in the crowd. The lobby seemed unusually busy today, with more people than usual milling around and a lot of guests dressed to the nines. There were men in tuxedos with brightly colored bow ties and cummerbunds, and women with "big hair" showing off their sequined and satin gowns.

"Is there a big party on or something?" Ellie asked one of the bellmen pushing a trolley full of luggage past her.

"Yes, ma'am. A wedding reception. Seems like the whole Greek community of Tampa Bay has come to the resort," said the bellman, grinning.

"Ah, right. By the way, I don't suppose you might know my aunt? She's an older lady with curly grey hair. She often wears these big floppy hats and bright outfits—"

"Oh yes, the mystery author," said the bellman, smiling broadly. "I know her. Had a nice chat with her the other day."

"Have you seen her around? I can't seem to find

her."

The bellman frowned. "I think I did see her earlier. She was over at the reception desk talking to one of the girls."

"Thanks!" Ellie hurried over to the reception counter and waited impatiently in line until she could speak to one of the staff there.

"Can I help you, ma'am?" one of the girls in a resort staff uniform said at last.

Hoping that it was the same girl that her aunt had been speaking to, Ellie described Aunt Olive again.

"Oh, yes, I remember her," said the girl brightly. "Mrs. Goldberg. She's one of our special long-term guests."

"Did she say if she was leaving the resort? Was she asking for you to arrange transport?" asked Ellie hopefully.

"No, nothing like that. She was asking about the Bronzed Babe bikini contest, actually," said the girl. "She wanted to know if she could have a copy of the contestants' registration details—you know, their names and contact addresses and such, which they had to give when they checked in. I said I had to check with Mr. Papadopoulos first and Mrs. Goldberg said that was fine and she'd be back to get the information later."

"When was this?"

The girl glanced at the clock on the wall behind her. "About... half an hour, maybe forty minutes ago?"

That would fit with the time Aunt Olive had left the villa. She had probably come to the reception to make the request—which was also probably why she'd left her mobile phone in the room, Ellie realized. She obviously hadn't intended to go far. But where had she gone afterwards? Why hadn't she returned to the villa?

Ellie thanked the girl and was about to turn away from the counter when the girl added: "I've got the information for Mrs. Goldberg here now. Would you like to have it?"

Ellie turned back to see the girl handing her a sheet of printed paper with the resort's letterhead at the top. "Oh, thanks. I'll give it to Aunt Olive."

She took the paper and glanced at it idly, then walked slowly away from the reception counter, still pondering Aunt Olive's whereabouts. She knew that it was silly to worry, that she should probably just return to the villa and wait until her aunt returned. After all, it wasn't the first time that Aunt Olive had taken off on an impulsive trip without warning or explanation. It was one of the things Ellie's parents found the most frustrating about their eccentric relative.

She looked up with a start as she nearly bumped into a distinguished-looking elderly gentleman who was hovering near the main lobby entrance. He was dressed in a white linen suit and had pomaded grey hair that matched his beautifully groomed moustache.

"Mr. Papadopoulos! I thought you were away," said Ellie, surprised to see the kindly owner of the Sunset Palms Beach Resort.

"I was, my dear. I went to visit a relative, but I had to return to oversee this wedding reception. The bride is the daughter of a good friend of mine, you see, and I am honored that they chose my resort to have the reception, so I wanted to make sure that everything goes smoothly." He glanced at the entrance. "I was told that the caterers would be arriving any minute with the wedding cake. It's my special gift to the happy couple and has been custom-made at great expense, so I'm anxious to make sure that they transport it carefully."

Mr. Papadopoulos gave a little smile. "I've known Anna since she was a little girl—it's strange to think of her getting married now." Then he looked anxious again as he added with a sigh, "I just hope this reception goes off without a hitch. It seems like there have been so many mishaps at the resort lately. I couldn't believe what my manager Mr. Anderson told me when I returned last night: a murder at the spa, sabotage, death threats..." He shook his head. "Who would have thought that so much could happen at an innocent bikini contest?"

"Yes, things have been a bit crazy the last few days," Ellie agreed.

"And I hear from my staff that your aunt has been helping the police with their investigation?"

"Oh... erm... yes, in a way," Ellie stammered,

wondering what exaggerations Aunt Olive had told the resort staff now.

"And what about you, my dear? I would have thought that you'd be by your aunt's side."

"What d'you mean?"

"Well, you don't seem to have accompanied Mrs. Goldberg to the marina."

"The marina? Aunt Olive's gone to the marina?"

Mr. Papadopoulos nodded. "I happened to step out of the front entrance for some fresh air ten minutes ago and I saw your aunt by one of the resort shuttles. She was asking the driver to take her to the marina. Normally, we require the shuttles to be at least half-full before they set off, but since Mrs. Goldberg is such a special guest, I told the driver he could ignore the usual rules and just take her first."

"Did Aunt Olive say what she was going to do at the marina?"

"No, although she did seem to be in a great hurry. I got the impression she was meeting somebody there—" Mr. Papadopoulos broke off as one of the girls from the reception desk beckoned to him. "You'll have to excuse me, my dear, but it seems that I'm wanted on the phone."

Left alone, Ellie pondered what Mr. Papadopoulos had told her. Why had Aunt Olive gone to the marina? Who had she gone to meet? Then she wondered what she should do. Now that she had some idea of where her aunt was, she felt slightly sheepish about her earlier panic. Maybe she had overreacted. If Aunt Olive had simply gone off to meet a contact, to get information for research, or maybe even just to meet Earl, then it would be silly for her to rush to the marina as well. Maybe she should go and find Blake, and explain why they should call off the search...

She was so deep in thought, she didn't see the two men carrying an enormous three-tiered cake come in through the lobby entrance.

"Oh! I beg your pardon," Ellie cried as she turned and nearly crashed into them. "I'm so sorry!"

"That's OK, ma'am." One of the caterers grinned at her. "You're not the first. We've had a couple of near-misses already."

"Why didn't you guys use the rear service entrance? Carrying a cake like this through a crowded lobby is just asking for accidents!"

They turned to see Mr. Anderson hurrying up to them. The resort manager had a well-deserved reputation for being fussy and demanding, and he was probably the worst person for the caterers to have encountered. Ellie felt slightly sorry for them as he gave them a tongue lashing, before calling some of the resort staff to help them. Within minutes, a trolley table was brought into the lobby and Mr. Anderson watched critically as the two caterers transferred the cake to the wheeled platform.

Ellie watched them push it toward the rear doors, wheeling the trolley table carefully out into the resort grounds on the way to the ballroom, with the cake towering between them. It really was a gorgeous creation, with each tier covered in sugar fondant and piped frosting, and an elaborate cake topper at the very top which read: "*Congratulations Georgios & Roxanna!*"

Then she froze, her eyes glued to the cake topper and, in particular, to the bride's name. She heard Mr. Papadopoulos's voice again saying: *"I've known Anna since she was a little girl—it's strange to think of her getting married now."*

Ellie snatched up the piece of paper she had been given by the receptionist and read the list of names once again:

Kimberley Lee
Nikki St. James
Amber Lopez
Sharlene Wolski
Roxanna Sinclair
Brandi Harris
Destiny Torres

This time, the fifth name on the list jumped out at her: *Roxanna Sinclair... Roxanna... Roxy...* Yes, "Roxy" was the most common shortened form of the name, but there were other possibilities too, like the bride who had chosen "Anna"...

Ellie suddenly recalled Ruth Blaise, the librarian at Riverfell High, talking about the girl who had been the victim of the cruel prank: *"I think it started with an A... something like Amy or Abby or Anna... maybe Amanda...*"

Ellie felt her heart give a lurch: *Could Roxy be the murderer?*

CHAPTER TWENTY-FOUR

Almost immediately, Ellie checked herself, laughing. *Don't be silly! What a ridiculous idea!* But now that it had popped into her head, the idea refused to go away. Instead, it took root and grew rapidly, until Ellie wondered how she hadn't seen the connections before. As Amber's roommate, Roxy would have had access to a supply of Benadryl from the packet in their shared bathroom, and she could have easily slipped something into Brandi's drink during the chaos of breakfast that morning at the resort buffet. Especially as she was seen as the "shy, quiet one," neither Gina nor the other girls would have paid her much attention.

Ellie recalled that her own treatment room at the spa had been sandwiched between Roxy's and Brandi's, and all the rooms on that side of the corridor looked out onto the spa garden, with French windows leading outside. Roxy could have slipped out of her own room and used the garden as an outdoor route into Brandi's room. That way, she wouldn't have needed to risk sneaking down the corridor and being seen. And the French windows in those treatment rooms were all unlocked; in fact, Ellie recalled the window in Brandi's room being slightly ajar when she'd gone in. She'd just assumed at the time that Monica, Brandi's beauty therapist, had left it open to let in the breeze, just like her own therapist had done in her room.

Now that Ellie thought about it, she remembered hearing heavy rustling outside her window, like a body moving through the foliage. When Mojito had shown up a few minutes later, she had just assumed that it had been the cat making that rustling noise outside... but what if it hadn't been Mojito? What if it had been Roxy creeping past, under the cover of the dense vegetation?

Then Ellie thought of something else: she had never seen Roxy without heavy foundation on her face. In fact, Roxy had even refused to have a facial that day at the spa, opting for a pedicure instead. Ellie had thought that it was low self-esteem and inexperience with make-up that had prompted Roxy to cake it on so heavily, but what if it had been intentional? What if the mask-like coverage was to hide scarring on her face... scarring that was the result of a tainted face cream that had caused chemical burns?

With her shy, timid personality, Roxy was just the type of student who might have been picked on by the "popular girls." Even if she looked like a swan now, she could have had an "ugly duckling transformation"—in fact, Ellie recalled Roxy mentioning having a weight problem in high school. Not that being overweight automatically led to being a victim, of course, but it certainly raised the possibility of Roxy being teased or mocked by the more "popular girls" and considered fair game for a cruel prank.

Then Ellie thought of the sweet, friendly girl she knew and she recoiled from the idea of Roxy being the murderer. It just seemed too improbable. Besides, hadn't Roxy herself received a threatening note? If she was the murderer, why would she have been threatened as well?

Because the best way to deflect suspicion was to look like a victim yourself, Ellie realized suddenly.

And it had worked. If there had been any suspicions about Roxy's involvement, they had been immediately pushed aside when the girl had given an Oscar-worthy performance as the hysterical victim of a death threat. Everyone's sympathies had instantly been with her, and no one had considered that she might have staged the whole thing herself.

Ellie remembered something else which sent a chill down her spine. Earlier that afternoon, when she and Aunt Olive had popped in to visit Roxy in her room, her aunt had talked about looking into the victim's background for answers. She'd mentioned contacting Brandi's high school and even getting hold of a copy of the dead girl's yearbook... and Roxy had heard every word. She had concealed her reaction well, but Ellie realized now that if Roxy was the murderer, she would have been worried at the prospect of Aunt Olive digging up the truth.

Roxy's picture would be in Brandi's yearbook, thought Ellie. *She might have looked very different in her teens, of course, but the resemblance could be enough for Aunt Olive to recognize her. Would she take that chance? And what about the faculty at Riverfell High, like Ruth Blaise the librarian? Roxy might have suspected that Aunt Olive would try to contact the school and would learn about Brandi's cruel prank on a fellow student. Would Roxy risk Aunt Olive connecting the dots? No,* thought Ellie with a sinking heart. *No, Roxy would make sure that Aunt Olive was silenced before she could pass on anything she discovered.* In fact, she—Ellie—had made things even worse by blithely telling Roxy that Aunt Olive "won't rest now until she's dug up every last thing she can find about Brandi's past."

I've got to keep Roxy away from Aunt Olive, Ellie thought with sudden urgency. Then she recalled Mr. Papadopoulos saying that her aunt had gone to meet someone at the marina. *Oh my God,* she thought. *Who? Roxy?*

Ellie hesitated, agonizing over what to do. If she could be sure that Roxy was still at the resort, she could relax. But it would take time to search for the girl and ascertain that she definitely wasn't here—at which point, it might be too late for Aunt Olive. No, better to just go straight to the marina and search there first. If she was wrong and Aunt Olive wasn't meeting Roxy, then it didn't matter. But if she was right...

Ellie had no proof, nothing other than a gut instinct, but somehow she couldn't shake the feeling that her aunt was in danger. She wondered where Blake was and cursed herself for leaving her own cellphone in the villa. In her haste to look for her aunt, she hadn't thought to grab her phone before she started searching, and now she had no way to contact Blake.

Never mind, I can go by myself, she decided.

Ellie rushed out of the front entrance, hoping that there might be another resort shuttle about to depart. Luck was with her: there was no shuttle in sight, but a taxi was just pulling up in front of the resort entrance and a young woman was getting out. Ellie rushed across to take over the taxi, then paused in surprise as she saw who was alighting from the car.

"Amber!" she cried. "Where have you been? Everyone's been looking for you."

The other girl shrugged. "I had some stuff to do. What's the big deal?"

"People were worried because you just disappeared without telling anyone where you were going."

Amber scowled. "We're not, like, in jail, you know. We can leave the resort if we want to. Gina's just a total control freak who wants to micro-manage everything we do all the time. And she's always on my case! It's not like I'm the only one leaving the resort. I saw Roxy driving out just now."

"Wait—you saw Roxy? Where? Where was she going?" asked Ellie urgently.

Amber gave her a strange look. "I passed her in my taxi as we were turning into the resort driveway. She was in her Honda on the other side of the road."

"Roxy has a car here?"

"Yeah. Most of us flew into Tampa International Airport but Roxy doesn't live that far away so she drove down."

"Hey, miss—are you getting in?" The taxi driver leaned over to look questioningly out of his window.

Ellie hesitated, then said, "Yes... one second, please!" She turned back to Amber and said urgently: "Listen, can you do me a favor? If you see Blake—I mean, Dr. Thornton—can you tell him that I've gone to the marina to look for my aunt?"

Before Amber had time to reply, Ellie hopped into the taxi and asked the driver to drive to the marina as quickly as possible.

When she was dropped off several minutes later, however, Ellie paused and looked uncertainly around, not sure where to start. The main boardwalk beside the marina entrance was brightly lit by the lights and neon signs of eateries and shops, but the rest of the marina was in relative darkness— particularly the long floating docks sticking out into the water.

It was a weekday night, but there seemed to be a live band in one of the restaurants and a sizeable crowd of people was milling around its entrance. Ellie hurried over but she could see at a glance that Aunt Olive wasn't amongst the couples and groups of people in the crowd. A quick look in the windows of the other eateries didn't reveal her aunt either. The shops were all closed now. That left the rest of the marina, where multiple yachts and other vessels were tied up along the floating docks. Ellie paused, scanning the rows and rows of moored boats, her heart sinking. She had no idea where to begin looking.

The catamaran, she thought suddenly. Yes, the catamaran that she and Aunt Olive had been on with the bikini contestants only a few days ago. It was as good a place to start as any other.

She took off at a jog, retracing her steps to the floating dock where they had all disembarked from the big Leopard 58 catamaran on that fateful day. It was on the outermost edge of the marina, due to the catamaran's greater size and need for a larger slip, and the whole area was dark and deserted. The music of the live band drifted over from the main boardwalk, together with the faint hubbub of talk and laughter, but it all sounded distant and surreal.

Ellie slowed her steps as she approached the big twin-hulled vessel, straining her eyes to see in the darkness. All around her, she could hear the soft slapping and sucking of the water against the sides of the docks, and the murmur of the wind blowing across the Intracoastal Waterway.

"Aunt Olive?" she called hesitantly.

A sudden movement on the deck of the catamaran caught her eye and she heard sounds of stumbling and a muttered oath. Someone was on board, at the bow of the boat. Ellie jumped onto the transom and climbed on board, nearly slipping and falling in her haste.

"Aunt Olive?" she called again, peering ahead.

Her heart skipped a beat as she saw a figure standing at the other end of the catamaran—it was Roxy. The young woman was hauling something that looked like a long, large sack. It was obviously heavy, because Ellie could hear the other girl panting with effort, and she also heard the slithering sound of something being dragged across the deck. For a fantastic moment, Ellie wondered if it was a dolphin or a seal.

No, she realized with a jolt of her heart. *It's a human body.* A limp body—dead or unconscious—that was being hauled to the edge of the boat. Ellie felt a sudden surge of fear as she thought of her missing aunt.

"Aunt Olive?" she cried. "Roxy, nooo!"

CHAPTER TWENTY-FIVE

Roxy froze, then swung around to face Ellie, still holding on to the body. Her motion caused the body's head to loll back against its shoulders, exposing the face to the light of a distant lamp, and Ellie's heart contracted. It was Aunt Olive.

"What have you done to my aunt?" she demanded, rushing across the deck toward them.

"STOP! DON'T COME ANY CLOSER!" cried Roxy sharply.

Ellie skidded to a stop a few feet away from the girl. She was relieved to see the faint rise and fall of Aunt Olive's chest. Her aunt might be out cold, but she was still alive.

Slowly, Ellie held up both hands in a placating gesture. "OK! OK, I won't come closer... but just let my aunt go."

Roxy glanced at the limp form of the old woman and gave a jeering laugh. "She thought she was so clever, but she didn't suspect me at all, until it was too late!"

"Did you tell her to meet you here?" asked Ellie, hoping to keep the other girl talking until she could think of a way to reach her aunt.

"Yeah. I knew I had to do something after I heard her talking this morning. No way was I going to let her dig up everything that happened at Riverfell High—I'm not living through that hell again! So I pretended to go off with Nikki, but as soon as we were, like, out of your sight, I left her and circled back to your aunt's villa. I wrote your aunt this note: 'I found a clue that everyone missed on the catamaran... meet me at the marina so I can show you.'" Roxy gave a self-satisfied smile. "It was so easy. I left the note outside the front door, knocked on the door, and then hid behind some bushes nearby. I saw your aunt's face when she came out and picked up the note. She looked so excited... the dumb old bat."

Ellie bristled but she held her tongue. The last thing she needed now was to antagonize Roxy.

"I knew your aunt would wanna think she's some kind of hotshot Miss Marple so she'd definitely come to meet me," Roxy continued. "So all I had to do was wait here at the catamaran and knock her out when she wasn't looking. Then I could throw her overboard and she would drown before anyone could save her.

Not that anyone would hear anything anyway out here, especially with that racket going on," she added, nodding in the direction of the main boardwalk and the sounds of the live band.

"But I'm here now," said Ellie quickly. "I know what really happened that day at the spa—you won't be able to hide the truth, whatever you do to Aunt Olive. So the best thing is to let her go."

Roxy scowled. "I could deal with you too—don't think I can't!"

"You won't get away with another two murders," said Ellie. "There would be too many questions, too many coincidences; people would start to wonder—"

"Hah! *People!*" Roxy gave another sneering laugh. "People are all such suckers! They're so easy to manipulate, if you know, like, the right buttons to press. Especially if you get them to feel sorry for you and think you're some poor, helpless little girl."

"You'd still never get away with it," insisted Ellie. "But I'm sure the authorities would be very understanding if you turned yourself in. Everyone will find out what happened to you at Riverfell High and they'll realize what Brandi did. They'll understand why you wanted revenge—"

"No! Girls like Brandi always get away with everything!" snarled Roxy. "Do you know she didn't even get punished back then for what she did? Yeah, she just got some random lecture from the principal about 'decent behavior' and then everyone just wanted to sweep it under the rug and move on. But what about *me*?" she demanded, her voice becoming shrill. "What about my face? How did they expect me to just go on, with a face like *this*?"

She grabbed the hem of her shirt and lifted it up, scrubbing one cheek violently. Then she turned her face to Ellie, who winced at what had been revealed. With the thick cover of foundation gone, Roxy's complexion was covered in red bumps and pitted scars.

"I thought they really wanted to help me," she said, her voice raw with emotion now. "I thought they were being nice to me for a change. The day before the prom, Brandi came up to me in the cafeteria and she was like: *'Hey girl—I noticed you got all these pimples on your cheeks. I've got this awesome cream which clears up breakouts in, like, a flash. You just use it overnight and the next day, your skin is clear and gorgeous!'* And she gave me this tub and told me to put a thick layer on my skin before bedtime." Roxy's face hardened at the memory. "It was all lies! They'd mixed in a super-strong solution of glycolic acid—the kind of stuff used in chemical peels—and they didn't care what it might have done to me. I was such a fool to believe them! But I never thought anyone could be so cruel. Even when I put it on my face and it really stung, I told myself it was just the cream working. But when I woke up the next morning and looked in the mirror..."

Roxy shuddered at the memory. Then she took a deep breath and stood up straighter. "But I'm done with being the victim now. And I'm not gonna let girls like Brandi get away with picking on others, just because they're pretty and popular." She tossed her hair back and gave Ellie a grim look. "That's one thing I learned from what happened at Riverfell High: if you want revenge, you gotta take care of it yourself. I swore then that I'd make Brandi pay, even if it took me years."

"You mean... you've been planning this since you left high school?" said Ellie disbelievingly.

"Hey, they say 'revenge is a dish best served cold,' right?" said Roxy with a smile. "And it was kinda good, actually. Everyone says you need a long-term goal, right? It really, like, helped me focus: I lost weight, I worked out, I learned to use make-up and dress better, I got myself a good job... and all along, I kept watching and waiting. Brandi never knew I was stalking her, of course—she's such a bimbo—but I knew everything that she was doing. And when I saw that she'd entered this bikini contest, I knew my chance had come. I applied to join the contest too." She paused, frowning slightly. "I was kinda worried that Brandi might recognize me, but I thought I was pretty safe. I've changed a lot since my high school days." She smiled bitterly. "And anyway, you know what? Brandi never even looked at me closely. She was so wrapped up in herself; she only ever looked at her own nails and hair and her stupid fake boobs."

Ellie stared at the girl in front of her. She couldn't believe that the shy, timid persona she'd known could be the front for such a cold, ruthless interior.

"How did you kill her?" she asked Roxy. "I'm guessing that you must have used the spa garden to sneak across to Brandi's room, but how did you get out of your own room without your therapist seeing? When the police questioned the staff, the girl who was doing your treatment swore that she'd never left the room."

"And she was telling the truth."

"But if she never left, how could you have sneaked out without her noticing?" demanded Ellie.

Roxy laughed. "I didn't try to stop her from noticing, dummy! I just got her to believe that she was seeing something else. I told her this sob story about how the contest was really strict and we weren't allowed to smoke, otherwise we'd be disqualified. And I've been trying to quit but I was so nervous and stressed, I was desperate for a cigarette... I got her feeling really sorry for me, and so when I asked if I could sneak out into the garden to have a quick smoke, she was, like, super nice and promised not to tell anyone, so I wouldn't get in trouble." Roxy smirked. "Of course, I didn't know if she'd keep her promise when she was questioned by the police, but I was pretty confident that she would. See, people aren't that hard to figure out. You just learn how they think and you can guess how they'll act in certain situations. I knew that she'd probably lie to the police 'cos she'd figure that it didn't matter, since I was unlikely to be the murderer anyway."

"And you sent yourself a fake death threat, didn't you?" asked Ellie. "You must have set up that doll and note in the room yourself that morning."

"Yeah, that was easy," said Roxy with an airy wave of her hand. "I just made sure Amber went down to breakfast first. And I stole the lipstick from the make-up bag they had at the photoshoots—I figured that way, they couldn't trace it back to me."

"So what about all the other things that happened? The accidents and acts of sabotage? Was that all down to you too?"

Roxy gave a humorless laugh. "Yeah, that was all me. I even tried to spread this rumor about a hex on the contest. I thought if there were, like, lots of accidents and stuff, then when the bad thing happened to Brandi, it wouldn't stand out, you know? Like, they'd think that all the girls were targeted and she just got unlucky."

She glanced sideways at the trampoline stretched across the twin hulls of the catamaran and Ellie followed her gaze. For some reason, the owner of the boat hadn't replaced the torn mesh fabric yet and it was still showing a gaping hole in the center.

"It was a shame Amber didn't get hurt or maybe even killed that day," said Roxy in a careless voice. "That would have looked even better. Like, it would have seemed *really* random when Brandi was later killed as well."

Ellie stared at the other girl in disgust and horror. Roxy's total lack of remorse and empathy was terrifying. *She's a real psychopath*, thought Ellie. She looked helplessly at her aunt, who was still slumped against Roxy's side. Could she possibly grab Aunt Olive and yank her out of Roxy's grasp? But even if she managed to do that, what next? With her aunt unconscious, there was no way to get her away from the catamaran. Aunt Olive couldn't walk on her own and she was too heavy for Ellie to lift and carry.

But I can't just leave Aunt Olive in Roxy's clutches, thought Ellie desperately. *She's such a nutter—who knows what she might do next?*

As if reading her mind, Roxy suddenly said: "Don't think about trying anything."

Ellie saw the other girl's knuckles whiten as her grip on Aunt Olive tightened. "Wait, Roxy—" she said, taking a step forward.

"KEEP BACK!" shouted Roxy, starting to look agitated.

Her flustered demeanor emboldened Ellie, who took another step forward. "I just want to help," she said, keeping her voice calm and measured. Slowly, she reached out toward Aunt Olive's limp body. "Look, why don't you let me take my aunt and then we can talk—"

Roxy reacted sharply, grabbing Aunt Olive under the armpits and heaving her up suddenly against the guardrail of the catamaran.

"No!" Ellie gasped, lunging forward.

It was too late. Roxy shoved the older woman's body over the guardrail and pushed, tipping her over.

Ellie screamed as she saw Aunt Olive roll over the edge of the catamaran and fall into the water below with a resounding splash. She rushed to the guardrail and peered frantically over at the black water around the boat. Faintly, she could see her aunt's body bobbing up to the surface. The water seemed to have roused Aunt Olive, but although she was normally a strong swimmer, now she was only moving feebly in the water.

"You bloody witch! What have you done to her?" Ellie demanded, glaring at Roxy.

Roxy gave a jeering laugh. "Don't worry—that knock on her head will make sure that she drowns quickly."

Ellie felt a boiling rage fill her. She swung her arm and punched Roxy in the face. Or at least, she tried to. She'd never been taught how to punch anyone before, and somehow those two classes of Body Combat at the gym didn't seem to help much. So she missed wildly. But her violent movement unbalanced her, sending her lurching forward to crash bodily into Roxy. The other girl reeled back, cursing, and tumbled backwards, falling onto the trampoline which was stretched out behind her. This would have been fine except for the torn hole still in the center of the mesh fabric. Roxy screamed and flailed her arms as she rolled sideways and fell through the hole into the water below.

Ellie had managed to yank herself back upright, so that she hadn't fallen onto the trampoline as well.

Now she whirled around to the guardrail again. She could see her aunt still struggling, but her movements were already getting weaker and she was starting to sink.

Ellie kicked off her shoes and stood poised at the edge of the catamaran, her heart hammering violently. The thought of jumping off the boat straight into the deep, black water below terrified her. She had only just gained confidence floating and "swimming" on her own without help. But that was in the lovely, warm turquoise water of the resort pool where she could always stand up again at any time. It was a totally different thing swimming in the deep, black water of the Intracoastal Waterway.

I can't do it, thought Ellie wildly. *It's too deep... and I can't reach the bottom... and they say there's sharks and even alligators in there. Oh God, I can't do it! I have to go and get help!*

But she knew that it would take too long to go for help. By the time she ran back to the main boardwalk, found someone who could swim, and convinced them to come back to help, it could be too late for Aunt Olive. Every minute she delayed, her aunt could sink deeper and drown...

I have to do it, thought Ellie. *There's no one to save Aunt Olive but me.*

She took a deep breath and jumped.

CHAPTER TWENTY-SIX

Ellie had never been so scared as she was during the fleeting few seconds when she jumped from the catamaran and fell through the air. Then she hit the water and plunged under, and the shock wiped all conscious thought from her mind. Instinct took over as she clawed her way back to the surface. She burst out with a gasp, panting and coughing, and paddled frantically, trying to tread water.

For a moment, panic filled her as she felt herself sinking again despite her efforts. She paddled even faster, kicking furiously in all directions, churning water around her. Water sloshed over her head and Ellie choked, feeling herself going under again.

I can't swim! she thought in terror. *I'm going to sink and drown!*

Then she thought of Blake and remembered his

calm, reassuring words during all those "swimming lesson dates" they'd had: "*Kicking too hard and too wildly just tires you out and makes you panic... need to relax and breathe normally...*"

Sucking in a shuddering breath, she forced herself to calm down, to kick slower and more deliberately, while moving her arms in sync through the water. To her surprise, instead of sinking even faster, she remained buoyant, bobbing gently up and down on the surface.

A wave of relief and elation swept through her. Ellie looked around with a clear head for the first time, searching for her aunt. A spurt of panic hit her again as she saw the top of Aunt Olive's head a short distance away. Her aunt had drifted out into the middle of the Intracoastal and was barely managing to keep herself afloat, her exhausted body sinking deeper and deeper in the water.

"Hold on, Aunt Olive! I'm coming!" shouted Ellie.

She gathered herself, then struck out toward her aunt. She swam with a disjointed mixture of breaststroke, dogpaddle, and random flailing around, but somehow it seemed to move her through the water. She arrived at Aunt Olive's side a few minutes later, breathless but jubilant.

"P-poppet?" Aunt Olive quavered as she struggled weakly. "Is...is that y-you?"

"Yes! I'm here, Aunt Olive! I've got you!" cried Ellie, reaching out to clasp her aunt's thin body.

She swung one arm around her aunt, pulling her

close, then turned to swim back toward the catamaran. But Ellie discovered that swimming whilst hauling another person was not easy. Aunt Olive's body felt like a dead weight and dragged in the water, pulling her down, so that she felt as if she was paddling frantically in place. She kicked and splashed for several minutes before she had to pause, panting and exhausted, and she was dismayed to see that they had barely moved a few feet.

And Aunt Olive seemed to be losing consciousness again. The older woman's body sagged even deeper in the water, her head drooping down. The sight put a fresh burst of fear in Ellie's heart and she began swimming again with renewed vigor, dragging her aunt with her.

At last, they reached one of the smooth twin hulls of the catamaran. Ellie threw a hand up, her numb fingers splaying against the gleaming white surface, but there was nothing to grip, nothing to hold on to. Ellie's heart sank. She looked up despairingly. The top of the catamaran was so far away! There was no way she could reach up and catch hold of the edge to haul herself up, nor any way she could lift Aunt Olive up—not without someone on deck to help. But there was no other way to scale the slippery vertical sides of the boat.

What am I going to do? Ellie wondered. She was nearly spent, her limbs weak and shaking from the effort of swimming and pulling her aunt's inert body.

Her chest heaved with deep, gasping breaths and her head spun from exhaustion. If they stayed here, she knew that she would not be able to keep Aunt Olive or even herself afloat forever. She remembered reading that people drowned more frequently from exhaustion than from not being able to swim and she understood now how that could happen. Right now, she was so sore and fatigued, it was all she could do not to just give up and let herself sink into the watery depths.

Then a weak voice spoke up next to her: "Th-the transom, p-poppet... the s-swim platform..." Aunt Olive lifted a shaking hand and pointed to the other end of the catamaran.

Yes, of course! Why hadn't she thought of it? Like all boats, the catamaran would have a swim platform attached to the transom at its stern, especially designed to make it easy for swimmers to climb back onto the boat. Ellie just had to find enough strength to drag her aunt down the length of the catamaran and around to the rear end, then haul herself out...

She didn't know how she did it—through sheer force of will if nothing else—but finally, they made their way down the whole length of the catamaran and around to the small, flat platform lowered to the water. Ellie's left arm, which was clamped around her aunt's body, was aching and felt as if it had been pulled out of its socket, but she hadn't let go, and now she pushed Aunt Olive toward the swim platform. But the older woman seemed too weak to haul herself out. In fact, she seemed to have passed out again and her head dipped dangerously into the water.

"Aunt Olive!" Ellie shouted, trying to shake her aunt. "Aunt Olive, wake up! We're almost there!"

But her aunt didn't respond. A fresh wave of fear washed over Ellie. She had been so preoccupied with getting them to the swim platform that she hadn't paid as much attention to keeping her aunt above the surface. Now she wondered if Aunt Olive might have inhaled some water. She needed to get the older woman out and give her first aid treatment! But if she let go of Aunt Olive to climb out herself first, her aunt might sink before Ellie had time to turn around and grab her to pull her up. Despair welled up in her and threatened to overwhelm her, making hot tears come to her eyes.

Then Ellie heard a familiar male voice:

"Ellie! Hold on!"

She looked up and her heart leaped as she saw Blake racing down the floating dock toward them. He leaped onto the transom and crouched on the swim platform, reaching down to haul Aunt Olive up. A minute later, Ellie felt strong hands grasp her gently under the armpits, then pull her, dripping, out of the water. She nearly sobbed with relief as Blake pulled her close and hugged her tightly for a second, before letting her go and turning to Aunt Olive.

Quickly, Blake laid the older woman on her back and checked her pulse and breathing, then he began giving her CPR, alternating between blowing into her mouth and giving her chest compressions. He worked swiftly and efficiently, with practiced movements, and as Ellie watched anxiously, she reminded herself that Blake used to be an ER doctor. *He's used to dealing with emergencies, with near-fatal accidents and life-threatening conditions... he would know how to save Aunt Olive... he has to!*

Suddenly Aunt Olive jerked and then began coughing and vomiting water everywhere, and Ellie felt herself go weak with relief. Blake continued to minister to her aunt a bit longer, gently turning her at last into the recovery position. Pulling his phone out of his pocket, he made a quick call, then he looked up at Ellie and gave her a reassuring smile.

"I've called for medical assistance. The paramedics should be here soon. But don't worry—I think your aunt is going to be OK."

Ellie sagged onto one of the leather seats on the aft deck. "Th-thank God you came, Blake," she said in a shaky voice. "I...I don't know if I could have held on much longer."

"What happened?" asked Blake. "Was there an accident?"

"No, Aunt Olive was hit on the head and then pushed off the catamaran by—"

Ellie broke off as she suddenly remembered Roxy. She'd completely forgotten about the girl in the panic to save her aunt.

"Roxy!" she cried. "I forgot all about her! She fell

in the water too."

She sprang up and scanned the water surrounding the boat. It was hard to see far in the darkened marina, but there was no sign of anyone— no head bobbing up, no figure swimming in the distance. Ellie's heart gave an uncomfortable lurch. Had Roxy drowned? The girl might have been a cold-blooded murderer, but Ellie still felt guilty for not thinking of her until now.

I couldn't have saved two people anyway, she told herself. *Even if I had seen Roxy in the water, I would have had to choose to rescue Aunt Olive first.*

Blake had stood up when she cried out and was now scanning the water beside her. "I can't see anyone," he commented. "But I remember Gina telling me that one of the requirements for the bikini contest entrants was that they should be strong swimmers, because if they won the Bronzed Babe modeling contract, they would have to pose in the ocean. So as long as she wasn't hurt, Roxy should be able to swim to shore. She might have climbed out somewhere on the other side of the marina." He turned to look at Ellie quizzically. "But why did she hit your aunt on the head and push her off the boat?"

Ellie took a deep breath. "Because she murdered Brandi and she didn't want Aunt Olive digging up the truth and telling the police."

Blake's eyes widened. "*Roxy* is the murderer? But how...? Why...?"

Before Ellie could answer, there was a soft groan

from next to them and they turned to see Aunt Olive trying to raise herself up into a sitting position.

"Aunt Olive!" cried Ellie, rushing over to crouch next to the older woman. "Take it easy—"

"Oh, don't fuss, poppet," said Aunt Olive, sounding much more like her old self. "I'm fine."

"You nearly drowned!" said Ellie. "You have to be careful."

Blake had crouched down next to them, and now he put a hand behind Aunt Olive's back to support her.

"Ellie is right: you've had a close call just now, and you need to give yourself time to recover," he said gently. He smiled at her. "How do you feel, Mrs. Goldberg?"

She looked up at him, her brown eyes twinkling. "Well, if it means that I get a kiss of life from a handsome doctor like you, I think I could handle being drowned every day!"

CHAPTER TWENTY-SEVEN

The police put out an alert for Roxy and she was caught as she was trying to leave the state. Ellie had wondered if there would be an indignant scene of surprise and denial, and whether she and Aunt Olive would become embroiled in an unpleasant game of "he said, she said." But to her surprise, once she was in custody, Roxy readily confessed to the murder as well as the attempt on Aunt Olive's life. In fact, she seemed almost proud, boasting about how she had masterminded the entire scenario and deceived everyone.

"She sounds like a very disturbed young lady," commented Aunt Olive as she and Ellie walked into the Sunset Palms resort lobby two days later.

"I just can't believe that I completely fell for her act," said Ellie with a sigh. "I mean, I always thought that I was a fairly good judge of character. This has really made me doubt myself."

"Don't blame yourself, dear," said Aunt Olive. "Psychopaths are well known for their abilities to charm everyone and maintain a double persona. There have been so many serial killers and murderers who committed their crimes whilst living perfectly normally amongst family, neighbors, and friends, and everyone was shocked when they found out the truth. Roxy was skilled at manipulating others and she knew exactly which buttons to push—"

"Yeah, she certainly knew how to push mine," muttered Ellie. "I completely fell for her 'shy, awkward outsider' act! She made me feel so sorry for her."

"Well, of course. It made her look like less of a threat in general, so that no one would consider her seriously as a suspect. Plus, we're more inclined to like people we feel sorry for and to see them in a positive light. Still, there's one who wasn't fooled by her act," added Aunt Olive with a smile, nodding in the direction of the reception desk.

Ellie turned to see a sleek black cat sitting at the end of the counter, daintily washing her face. "Mojito?" she said, puzzled.

"Yes, don't you remember, poppet? The day we visited Roxy in her room and you were carrying Mojito. As soon as Roxy tried to take her, Mojito hissed and growled, then she wriggled free and ran."

"Oh... but surely that could have been a coincidence?" said Ellie. "I mean, we thought Mojito just didn't like the smell of the sunscreen."

"Perhaps," said Aunt Olive. "But I think animals have a sixth sense for things sometimes—they can pick up vibes which we humans can't and see through an act to the true person within."

"You know, maybe you're right," said Ellie slowly. "I've just remembered something! That day when we were on the catamaran and the girls were doing their photoshoot, Hemingway was being especially difficult around Roxy. He turned his back to her and refused to even look at her. When she put out a hand to him, he lunged at her and tried to bite her. I was really surprised because I'd never seen Hemingway behave like that. He's cheeky but he's not aggressive."

"Well, there you are," said Aunt Olive. "Animals always know."

"Shame he couldn't have just told me directly," joked Ellie. "Although come to think of it... he did call Roxy 'NASTY BROCCOLI.'"

"Oh yes, I remember that," said Aunt Olive, chuckling. "And I've seen him flinging pieces of broccoli at guests in the lobby, you know. His aim is amazingly accurate. I'm not surprised they had to give up trying to get him to eat it."

"Yes, but my point is—everyone just thought Hemingway was referring to the vegetable, but maybe he uses that as a general term for anything or anyone he doesn't like."

"Hmm, you could be right, poppet. Parrots are very intelligent and can make abstract associations. Maybe he was trying to tell you that Roxy is a 'nasty' person and that was his way of saying it." Aunt Olive paused in the middle of the lobby and looked around, sighing with pleasure. "Ahh... it's good to be back. I thought that doctor at the hospital was never going to release me! Honestly, I kept telling him that I felt fine—"

"They had to keep you in for observation. You *did* nearly drown, you know, Aunt Olive."

"Oh, fiddle-faddle! Swallowing a bit of water never hurt anyone," said Aunt Olive, waving a hand dismissively.

Well, at least it doesn't look like I'll have to worry about Aunt Olive suffering from any kind of post-traumatic experience after her ordeal, reflected Ellie wryly.

They had just returned from the hospital where Aunt Olive had been discharged after a forty-eight-hour stay. Ellie glanced again at her aunt, pleased to see that she really did seem to be none the worse for wear after her trials at the marina. In fact, Aunt Olive had insisted on stopping at a hair salon on their way back from the hospital and getting a new dye and trim.

"Nothing like a near-death experience to make you feel like a makeover," Aunt Olive declared, fluffing her hair and admiring her new blue rinse in the reflection of one of the lobby windows. "It was mortifying having Earl visit me in hospital and seeing me in that dreadful gown and with all those wires to the cardiac monitor! I must make sure that I wow him the next time I see him."

"I think he was pretty wowed anyway," said Ellie, looking down at the enormous bouquet of roses that Earl had brought to the hospital and which she was helping her aunt carry back to their villa. "I don't think any patient there had ever received such a huge bunch of roses!"

"Yes, isn't he sweet?" said Aunt Olive. She gave Ellie an impish look. "Maybe he's not a bad option for Husband Number Two."

"Aunt Olive!" gasped Ellie, staring at her aunt. "Are you serious?"

Her aunt gave a mysterious smile and didn't answer. Instead, she walked over to the other side of the lobby where several staff members were putting up tinsel and decorating an enormous artificial pine tree with ribbons and baubles.

"I'm surprised to see them putting up the decorations so late—Christmas is only a couple of weeks away," said Aunt Olive.

"It feels so odd having a Christmas tree when there's blazing sunshine and blue skies outside," Ellie said, watching the staff members work. "It just doesn't feel like the Yuletide season at all!"

"Would you prefer some grey English skies and wind and rain?" asked Aunt Olive with a chuckle.

"Oh no, I'm looking forward to enjoying a beach

Christmas," said Ellie hastily. "It'll be a novelty. I suppose it's just the associations that one's used to; you know, the cold and log fires, roasting chestnuts and snow, turkey and Christmas pudding—"

"I'm sure the resort restaurants will be dishing up plenty of Christmas turkey, and all the other traditional treats," said Aunt Olive. "And you might find that you enjoy some of the American favorites, like eggnog, too. Plus I've heard that the Sunset Palms New Year's Eve party is legendary."

"Mmm..." said Ellie, her mind drifting to the time beyond Christmas and New Year's, when she would have to head home.

When the unexpected invitation had come from Aunt Olive, back in October, to join her in Florida, Ellie had welcomed the break from the rut she had fallen into. The extended vacation in the Sunshine State had been a chance to finally have the "adventure in a foreign land" that she'd always wanted and to escape from the mundane routines of her life in London. But she'd always known that the vacation couldn't last forever—that at some point, she would have to return and face the same question that she'd been grappling with before she left: what was she going to do with her life?

In spite of her defensive answers to her parents whenever they criticized her, Ellie knew in her heart that drifting from one temping job to another wasn't a career. It wasn't something she wanted to spend the rest of her life doing. The problem was, Ellie didn't really know *what* she wanted to spend the rest of her life doing. Unlike her sister Karen, who had every last minute of her future already mapped out (and probably the minute details of her funeral too), Ellie had no professional aspirations in medicine, accountancy, or law, no burning desire to run her own company, no wish to enter politics or work in fashion or open a restaurant... or even be "just a housewife."

Aunt Olive gave Ellie a shrewd look, as if reading her thoughts, and said: "What are you planning to do when you return to London?"

Ellie sighed. "I don't know. Look for a job, I suppose," she said without much enthusiasm.

"Well, I've been thinking and I have an idea," said Aunt Olive, her eyes gleaming. "How would you like a job, poppet... as my personal assistant?"

Ellie blinked at her aunt. "Your assistant?"

Aunt Olive nodded. "Yes, I've been thinking for a while now of hiring an assistant. Someone to help me with research for my books and other general administration, like my social media and book promotion activities. I want someone who is resourceful and persistent, who can think outside the box and do things on her own initiative." Aunt Olive smiled at Ellie. "Watching you investigate these murders at the resort in the past few weeks, I've been very impressed, my dear. I think you have just the natural talents I'm looking for."

"Oh... I... thank you," Ellie stammered.

"You'd have to be willing to travel, of course, as I move around between Europe and America regularly, so you won't be able to remain living in the U.K. full-time. Plus you'll be spending a lot of time with me," Aunt Olive continued. "I suppose what I'm really looking for is what would have been called a 'lady's companion' in the old days—with a dash of secretary and private investigator thrown in," she added, her eyes twinkling. "So... what do you think, poppet?"

Ellie was lost for words. "I..."

"You don't have to give me your answer now," said Aunt Olive. "In fact, I want you to mull things over until at least the new year. This isn't a decision you should rush into. But do think about it and let me know before you return home." She paused, then added with a wink: "Maybe it'll just be a short trip to collect your things and you'll be back here with the sunshine and ocean and white sand beaches soon. I can think of one handsome American doctor who would be very happy about that."

Ellie blushed but, before she could reply, there was a flapping of wings and a flurry of feathers, and an enormous scarlet macaw landed on her shoulder. He gave an ear-piercing squawk that caused Ellie to wince, then began to nibble her earlobe.

"Stop it, Hemingway," Ellie gasped, giggling and trying to twitch away from the parrot. "That tickles!"

"Here's another one who's going to miss you terribly," Aunt Olive observed, watching them. "I don't think I've seen him bond to any other guest so quickly."

"Well, I can't believe I'm saying this, but I *am* going to miss Hemingway a lot when I leave," said Ellie, laughing and shaking her head. "He's an absolute terror, but somehow he's grown on me."

"*PANTS ON!*" croaked Hemingway.

Aunt Olive stared. "Did the parrot just tell me to put my pants on?"

Ellie laughed. "No, he's just repeating part of a phrase I taught him the other day. I was trying to teach him 'liar, liar, pants on fire' but he seems to have only picked up part of it."

Hemingway cocked his head as he listened to Ellie speaking, then he said again: "*PANTS ON!*"

Aunt Olive guffawed. "I hope he's not going to fly around the resort now telling all the guests to put their pants on."

Before Ellie could reply, there was a loud commotion on the other side of the lobby. A man and a woman burst through the main entrance. They were surrounded by a crowd of paparazzi, all yelling questions and thrusting microphones in their direction. Flash bulbs exploded and boom mics waved wildly around as photographers and cameramen scurried to keep the couple in their sights. Hemingway screeched and flapped his wings, adding his own raucous voice to the din.

Ellie and her aunt drifted over to see what the fuss was about, with Hemingway still perched on Ellie's shoulder, excitedly watching the crowd around them.

Ellie stood up on tiptoe to peer over the heads of the crowd and was surprised to recognize the young woman as Amber and the young man standing beside her as Ted Baxter.

A reporter jumped forward and shoved a microphone at Amber's face: "Miss Lopez! Miss Lopez! Is it true that Don Palmer has been arrested for sexual assault—all because of you?"

CHAPTER TWENTY-EIGHT

Amber tossed back her glorious mane of auburn hair, placed a hand on her hips, and looked straight at the cameras, a cool smile playing at the corners of her lips.

"Yes," she said. "With the help of Ted Baxter from the *Tampa Daily News*, I'm exposing Don Palmer for the sexual predator that he is. Ted will be publishing an in-depth investigation into Palmer's history of sexual abuse, which will show you just how much that man belongs in jail. I'm not the first girl that Don Palmer has done this to—but I'm going to make damned sure that I'm the last!"

"But there have been accusations against Mr. Palmer in the past and he has never been charged—"

"That's because he always managed to spin a good

story and pay people off," said Amber. "But he's not going to talk or buy his way out of things this time! Plus, I have something that the other girls never had: I have proof."

There were gasps from the crowd.

"Proof? What proof?"

"Miss Lopez! Are you saying you have hard evidence of his offenses?"

"Are we talking video footage? Photographs?"

Amber waited until the clamor had subsided before saying: "I have everything: video footage showing Don Palmer trying to molest me; audio of his words implicating himself." She gave a satisfied nod. "Ohhh yes... after that first time when he made a pass at me, I made sure I was wired up and covered by a hidden camera when I was next alone with him and he provided the rest himself."

"Isn't that considered entrapment?" one of the reporters asked.

Amber narrowed her eyes at him. "Entrapment is not a valid defense if the defendant intended to commit the crime and you simply provided a means for them to do so." She turned to look slowly around the crowd, fixing each reporter with her gaze. "And believe me, Don Palmer intended to sexually assault me."

A silence greeted her cool, powerful statement, before a new uproar erupted as the reporters all surged forward again with more questions. Ellie watched Amber with a mixture of awe and admiration. The girl looked magnificent, standing there under the glare of the flashlights and cameras, her head held high, her face beautiful and confident as she answered the questions fired at her.

"Never mind the Bronzed Babe modeling contract—that girl is going to become the face of a movement," said Aunt Olive, watching her as well. "She'll be on the cover of *Time* magazine next."

"Well, good for her!" said a voice next to them. "This is a bigger prize than winning any stupid bikini contest."

Ellie turned to see Sandy O'Brien standing next to them, her eyes also on Amber.

"Hah! I was right all along: I told you Don Palmer was a lecherous rat," said Sandy smugly.

"*RAT!*" screeched Hemingway.

"Didn't I say he was abusing one of the bikini contestants?" Sandy said. "I just got a small detail wrong: I got the wrong girl. It wasn't Brandi that he tried to grope; it was Amber."

And he didn't murder her; he ended up arrested by her, thought Ellie. *That's a lot more than a small detail.* Still, she kept her mouth shut and stood politely beside Aunt Olive as Sandy said her goodbyes.

"My work here is done," said the activist with a satisfied sigh. "It's been a really productive few days. I even convinced one of the spa technicians to join me at the next protest I'll be attending! Monica told me that she never thought she wanted to be an activist for feminism, but after her experience with Don Palmer, she's determined now to—"

"Wait, what experience?" asked Ellie.

Sandy raised her eyebrows. "Didn't you know? Apparently, Palmer tried to grope Monica during a massage and, when she freaked out, he offered her money to keep quiet about it rather than report it to the spa manager. She's paying off a lot of student debt and it was a big sum, so she accepted. But afterwards, she started hating herself, especially when Palmer kept bringing it up whenever they met again. It was really starting to get to her; she just couldn't live with her conscience..."

Ellie thought suddenly of the way Monica had seemed preoccupied by dark thoughts when she'd seen the beauty therapist walking past the pool deck. Now it all made sense.

"...and she told me everything. I think it was a relief for her to have someone to confide in," Sandy was continuing. "I told her she should return the money and report him. We were just planning the best way to do that when the news came in about Palmer's arrest. But Monica told me that talking to me had really made her feel empowered and she was interested in joining me at some activist events." Sandy smiled with pleasure.

"Good on her," said Aunt Olive, adding with a wink: "You've got your first apprentice, Sandy."

The other woman laughed, then she said: "Well, I'm checking out today and heading home—"

"*THERE'S NO PLACE LIKE HOME*!" squawked Hemingway.

Sandy laughed and reached out to stroke the parrot's brilliant scarlet feathers. "You know, this guy's beginning to grow on me." She turned to Aunt Olive and held out her hand. "It's been great meeting you, Olive. Any time you're down in my neck of the woods, give me a holler. I could take you to some great protests!"

"That sounds fabulous," said Aunt Olive enthusiastically.

"Yeah, I'll show you what real American hospitality looks like. None of this fancy tourist crap," said Sandy, shooting a scornful look at the lobby around them.

Aunt Olive chuckled. "Well, I have to confess, Sandy, I was quite surprised to find you having a holiday here. I wouldn't have thought a resort like this would be quite your cup of tea."

"Oh, I wouldn't have come, except that I got the ticket and invite. Who's gonna turn down an all-expenses-paid stay at a beach resort, right?"

"I beg your pardon?" said Aunt Olive, looking surprised. "You mean you didn't book the stay yourself?"

"'Course not! Why would I spend my hard-earned cash to come to a place like this?" said Sandy scornfully. "But my momma always said: 'don't look a gift horse in the mouth.' So when the packet arrived with the details of my stay, all paid up, and a plane

ticket too... well, I decided to come and check it out."
She rubbed her hands with glee. "Even better when I
looked at the brochures and information included,
and found out that there was a bikini contest being
held here! I made sure to pack all my protest gear."

Ellie stared at her, a suspicion beginning to form
in her mind. "And you have no idea who might have
paid for your stay?"

Sandy smirked. "Well, I kinda found out by
accident, actually. I was talking to one of the girls at
the reception desk—you know, checking what was
included in my package—and she started saying how
sweet it was that I had this secret admirer who'd
booked me such a great vacation. Then she looked
horrified and apologized for slipping up. See, she
wasn't supposed to tell me; it was meant to be a big
secret. Naturally, I started badgering her, and in the
end she admitted that it was some guy called 'Mr. G.
Ross' who'd made the booking for my room." Sandy
waggled her eyebrows. "Well, I don't know any Mr.
Ross but I sure do know a *Miss* Gina Ross."

"Gina?" said Aunt Olive incredulously. "But why
on earth would she want to pay for you to stay at the
resort?"

"I have an idea and I'm going to ask her if I see
her," declared Sandy. Then her gaze went across the
lobby and she smiled. "Aha! Talk of the devil..."

"*THE DEVIL!*" cried Hemingway, raising one claw.
"*OH BOLLOCKS!*"

Ellie turned to see Gina enter the lobby from the

rear double doors that led out to the main resort grounds. She was accompanied by Blake and she was looking flirtatiously up at him, a coy smile on her lips, as she talked animatedly. Then she caught sight of Ellie, Aunt Olive, and Sandy O'Brien, and her face darkened. For a moment, she looked as if she might detour around the other side of the lobby to avoid them but, before she could turn away, Sandy rushed up to her. Aunt Olive went with her and Ellie reluctantly followed, Hemingway still perched on her shoulder.

"Miss Ross! I wanted to thank you before I leave," Sandy cried.

Gina regarded her warily. "I'm sorry? For what?"

"For your generous gesture! It was so kind of you to pay for my stay."

Gina's expression went blank. She took a step back from Sandy and said, "I'm sorry. You... you must be mistaken."

"Nope! I know it was your name on my booking. The resort staff told me. And it was so thoughtful of you to include all that information about upcoming events at Sunset Palms, including the bikini contest—"

"I... I really don't know what you're talking about," said Gina quickly. "I think you've got me mixed up with someone else. Ross is a fairly common name."

"Oh, I don't think so," said Sandy, looking like she was enjoying herself. "But don't be coy—there's no embarrassment in being a secret member of the sisterhood."

"The... the *what*?" Gina blinked at her.

Sandy wagged a finger at her. "I know you're a closet feminist! You didn't want anyone to know, but you organized for me to come to Sunset Palms, didn't you? And you provided all the information on Don Palmer's disgusting bikini pageant, because you knew that I would take up the torch for you." Sandy gave Gina a complacent smile and patted her shoulder. "Don't worry, you're not the first to have to hide her support of the feminist movement. There have been others before you who have had their hands tied in public but who have supported us in secret. Just providing me with the means to be here so I could draw attention to the ugly reality of the bikini contest was good enough! You have done your part for the sisterhood!"

"I... no... you've got things wrong," stammered Gina.

But Sandy was no longer listening. Whirling, she marched away. Aunt Olive hurried after her, and the two women could be heard eagerly discussing the best types of bras to burn as they walked together out of the lobby entrance.

CHAPTER TWENTY-NINE

There was a horrible, awkward silence after Sandy and Aunt Olive had left. Blake stood staring at Gina, who was still trying to regain her composure, and Ellie shifted uncomfortably from foot to foot, wishing that she had had the presence of mind to follow her aunt and Sandy away. Hemingway didn't help, bobbing up and down on her shoulder and croaking loudly:

"MY MAMA ALWAYS SAID LIFE WAS LIKE A BOX OF CHOCOLATES. YOU NEVER KNOW—"

Ellie groaned inwardly and hastily reached up to clamp her hand over the parrot's beak.

Blake spoke up at last. "Is it true?" he asked. "Did you secretly organize for Sandy O'Brien to come stay at the resort? Tell me the truth, Gina!"

Gina hesitated, then she raised her chin and said,

"Yeah, it's true. So what?"

"*So what?*" Blake stared at her, his eyes wide and disillusioned. "When I asked you, you said the only thing you lied about was your alibi at the spa. You said all you did was sneak into the changing room to place some of Sandy's flyers in the girls' bags. You swore to me that you weren't responsible for anything else that had happened... And now I find that you didn't just take advantage of Sandy's sudden appearance—you engineered the whole thing!"

Instead of looking chastened or ashamed, Gina gave Blake a defiant look. "OK, so I stretched the truth a bit—what's the big deal? It's not like I hired someone to put on a fake act. Sandy O'Brien really *is* a feminist activist who protests against beauty pageants. I just... helped her realize that there was one going on here at the Sunset Palms and made it easier for her to make her opinions known."

"But not because you're a secret feminist," said Blake, looking at her in disgust. "You did it all just to create controversy and get publicity for the contest."

Gina tossed her sleek blonde hair over her shoulder. "That's hardly a crime! Look, honey, I'm in the business of creating successful events. That means getting PR, getting hype on social media, getting media coverage... do you realize how hard it is to do that these days? There's so much competing for the public's attention. You have to use any means at your disposal to grab the headlines."

Blake stared at her. "I always knew that you were ambitious, Gina, but I never thought you'd be this ruthless and manipulative. Now I'm beginning to wonder if I ever really knew you."

Gina's lips curled and she pointed at Ellie, saying contemptuously, "Oh, unlike Little Miss Nancy Drew here, right? Of course, *she's* a totally open book."

"Leave Ellie out of this," Blake snapped. "This isn't about her—it's about you and me. It's about trust. I defended you, Gina. I trusted you when you said you were telling me the truth." He shook his head. "And now I find that I stood up for someone who's proud of being a liar."

"*LIAR!*" squawked Hemingway suddenly, leaning forward from Ellie's shoulder to eyeball Gina. "*LIAR! LIAR! PANTS ON FIRE!*"

Gina flushed to the roots of her hair and looked as if she wanted to throttle the parrot.

Ellie groaned silently, not knowing whether to laugh or cry. "Erm... I'm just going to take Hemingway out... to... to get some fresh air," she stammered, backing away from Blake and Gina.

Turning, she hurried out of the rear double doors which led into the main resort grounds. Hemingway screeched indignantly as he struggled to stay perched on her shoulders, spreading his wings to balance himself. Ellie finally slowed as she reached the edge of the pool deck, where a path led out onto the open beach. She kicked off her sandals and padded barefoot across the sand dunes between the leaning palm trees. A strong wind was blowing in from the Gulf and sweeping across the beach. It whipped Ellie's hair back from her face and lifted Hemingway up into the air. He flapped his wings, riding the current, as he flew next to her.

Ellie came to a stop at last next to two palm trees with a hammock strung between their trunks and Hemingway landed next to her, clinging vertically to one of the palm tree trunks.

"Bloody hell, Hemingway," Ellie said, looking at the parrot wryly. "Talk about bad timing! Did you have to finally get that phrase right *then*?"

"*NASTY*," said Hemingway, ruffling his feathers. "*NASTY BROCCOLI.*"

Ellie snorted with laughter. "Well, just between you and me, Hemingway, I think you're right: Gina *is* nasty broccoli."

"*MIAOW?*"

Ellie looked down to see Mojito slinking out of some inkberry bushes nearby and strolling up to them.

"Weren't you in the lobby just now?" said Ellie, reaching down absentmindedly to rub the cat's ears. "How do you get around the resort so quickly?"

Mojito purred loudly and butted her head against Ellie's knee.

"I'm going to miss you too," said Ellie with a rueful smile.

She sighed as she straightened and looked out across the beach at the sparkling water and the wide blue sky above. The fact that she was going to leave all this and head home to England in a few weeks was really beginning to sink in. Suddenly, she didn't want to go—not just because she didn't want to have to go back to the tedious reality of a boring nine-to-five job, but because there were things here, people here, that she was really going to miss. The Sunset Palms Beach Resort wasn't just a "vacation place" to escape to anymore—it had become a new way of life and the people here had become new friends and family.

There's a way I can keep all of this in my life, though...

Ellie thought of Aunt Olive's offer and felt a thrill of excitement. It would be a huge change and she wasn't sure how she would deal with the constant travelling, not to mention spending so much time with her aunt on a permanent basis... but surely it couldn't be worse than going back to England to work a dead-end job while living with her parents?

An excited chattering sound from Hemingway made her look up and she followed the parrot's gaze to see a tall male figure step onto the sandy path leading from the edge of the landscaped resort grounds to the beach. It was Blake. He had his hands thrust into his pockets and his head down as he walked. From the deep frown creasing his brow, it looked like he was immersed in distasteful thoughts.

Ellie wondered if she should call out to him. It looked like he had just finished the unpleasant conversation with Gina and might want some time alone. But even as she hesitated, Blake glanced up and caught sight of her. A broad smile spread across his handsome features and he quickened his steps, coming across the sand dunes toward her.

"Hi..." Ellie looked up at him shyly.

"Hi." Blake stopped next to her and cleared his throat, saying gruffly, "I... I'm sorry you got caught up in the stuff with Gina—"

"Oh no, I didn't mind," said Ellie quickly. "I mean... there's nothing to apologize for."

"But there is. I didn't believe you when you told me that Gina was hiding something; I was probably too harsh on you." Blake's mouth twisted bitterly. "I can't believe I defended her and accused you of being jealous—"

"It's not your fault," said Ellie, putting a soothing hand on his arm. "You couldn't have known and, in a way, it was very noble of you to defend Gina out of loyalty."

"*Blind* loyalty," said Blake, looking disgusted with himself.

Ellie gave him a sheepish grin, trying to lighten the mood. "And you weren't wrong—I *was* jealous of Gina."

Blake glanced up, his eyes softening. "You have no reason to be, you know."

Ellie felt her heart flutter at the look in his eyes. She found that she couldn't tear her gaze away as Blake moved closer, until their bodies were almost touching. Hemingway bobbed his head excitedly, then leaned towards them and made exaggerated kissing noises.

"*KISSY... KISSY... KISSY!*" he squawked.

It killed the moment. Ellie shot a dirty look at the bird, wanting to throttle him herself now. She couldn't look at Blake and she could feel a furious blush heating her cheeks. Then she heard Blake chuckle. He reached a gentle finger under her chin and tipped her face back up to his.

"Ever since that day I met a pretty English girl running through the waves on this beach... there's been no one else," Blake said, his brown eyes tender as he looked down at her.

Ellie caught her breath. "I... I feel the same way."

Blake raised his eyebrows. "You met an English girl too?"

"Idiot!" laughed Ellie, giving him a playful smack on the arm.

Then, before she could say anything else, Blake caught her in his arms and kissed her until she was breathless. When at last they broke apart, Ellie stared up at him in a dreamy daze. She'd thought that the first kiss they'd shared, on the night they went to the fish shack, was pretty special, but this... She didn't think that any man had made her feel the way Blake did. Then a shadow crossed her face as she thought suddenly of saying goodbye to him in a few weeks' time.

"What is it?" asked Blake. "Is something wrong?"

Ellie sighed and drew slightly out of his arms. "No, nothing's wrong. Just... well, you know I'm only in Florida on vacation, don't you?"

Blake nodded. "You've always said that you're planning to return home in the new year." His eyes searched her face. "Have you changed your mind?"

"No... yes... well, I don't know," stammered Ellie. "I've always just put off thinking about it, and anyway, I never expected things to... erm... well, get serious between us," she added with a shy smile. "But actually, my aunt offered me a job this morning—to remain with her as a sort of personal assistant, helping her with her book research and social media and things. I would have to be prepared to travel a lot and live 'on the road' with her all the time... sort of like a modern-day 'lady's companion,' I guess."

"And what did you say?"

Ellie shrugged helplessly. "I haven't given her a decision yet. I mean, I was dreading the thought of returning to my old life in dreary old England and this would be a way to escape all that, to have the exciting, adventurous life that I'd always dreamt of."

"But?" asked Blake.

Ellie sighed. "I don't know. I always thought that I'd jump at the chance of something like this, but now that it's happened... It's weird. A part of me is unsure. It *would* be a huge change from all I've ever known. And while it's been wonderful here at the resort with Aunt Olive... well, it might be different

271

when it's permanent. Then it wouldn't just be a fun escape for a few weeks' vacation, you know—it would become my life." She hesitated, then said, lifting her eyes up to his: "But it would be a way to see *you*, whereas if I go back to England—"

"Ah, well, you're not the only one who's been making plans," said Blake, a smile hovering at the corners of his mouth. "I fully expected you to be going back in January so... I've been exploring the possibility of a locum job in London."

Ellie furrowed her brow. "A locum job?"

"A locum doctor takes over temporarily when a physician needs to take extended time off for some reason, such as sickness, or just to help when a hospital is short-staffed. Sort of like substitute teachers. There are a lot of locum positions on offer in the U.K. It's a good way to try working and living in another country, without committing to a permanent contract."

Ellie stared. "You mean... you're willing to move to England? For me?"

"*FOR ME?*" cooed Hemingway. "*FOR ME?*"

Blake smiled at her. "I think we've got something special between us, don't you? I don't want to throw it away... so yes, I'm willing to move across the Atlantic if it means I can be with you and give 'us' a chance."

Ellie felt a rush of emotion. She reached up and hugged Blake close. "Thank you," she whispered.

"So don't worry about me," said Blake. "Make your

decision based on your own feelings. I'll be there, whatever you decide to do." He grinned and squeezed her hand. "Here in Florida... over in England... or anywhere else in the world you decide to go in search of 'adventure'... I'll be looking forward to it."

Ellie gave him an impish look. "Even if there's a murder or two?"

Blake laughed and gathered her in his arms again. As Ellie snuggled close, she saw Hemingway watching them with his head cocked to one side. She smiled at the parrot and said: "Hey Hemingway, did you learn the line from *The Terminator*? Hasta la vista—"

The parrot bobbed his head eagerly. *"HASTA LA VISTA, BABY!"*

"Yes," said Ellie, chuckling. "But you forgot the most important part: *I'll be back!"*

THE END

ABOUT THE AUTHOR

USA Today bestselling author H.Y. Hanna writes fun cozy mysteries filled with clever puzzles, lots of humor, quirky characters - and cats with big personalities! She is known for bringing wonderful settings to life, whether it's the historic city of Oxford, the beautiful English Cotswolds or the sunny beaches of coastal Florida.

After graduating from Oxford University, Hsin-Yi tried her hand at a variety of jobs, including advertising, modelling, teaching English, dog training and marketing... before returning to her first love: writing. She worked as a freelance writer for several years and has won awards for her novels, poetry, short stories and journalism.

A globe-trotter all her life, Hsin-Yi has lived in a variety of cultures, from Dubai to Auckland, London to New Jersey, but is now happily settled in Perth, Western Australia, with her husband and a rescue kitty named Muesli. You can learn more about her and her books at: www.hyhanna.com.

Join her Readers' Club Newsletter to get updates on new releases, exclusive giveaways and other book news!

https://www.hyhanna.com/newsletter

ACKNOWLEDGEMENTS

A big thank you to my beta readers, Kathleen Costa and Connie Leap, for their invaluable feedback on this manuscript and the whole series. I'm indebted to them and to my editor for helping to make sure that the American characters are portrayed as authentically as possible. I am also very grateful to the rest of my publishing team for being so understanding and fitting in with my ever-changing schedule during a difficult year.

And lastly, to my husband, who has been my rock with his unwavering support, encouragement and belief in me—I could never have done it without him.

Printed in Great Britain
by Amazon